Why did you bring Mother?

Joy Viney

Mother continues her travels - a sequel to
'... and Mother came too'

Love from

Joy

SUMMERSDALE

Summersdale Publishers
46 West Street
Chichester
West Sussex
PO19 1RP

A CIP catalogue record for this book is available from the British Library.

ISBN 1 902320 11 5

Printed in Great Britain

Illustrated by Sue Millar Smith

Dedicated to Dianne Hood

for her encouragement and help

Contents

The Characters

Joy - me, I've written this book

Tom - my husband, doesn't like travel and wonders why anybody else does

Simon - my son who does, and who works abroad anyway
Jennie - his wife
Elizabeth - their daughter
Adam and Peter - their sons

Amanda - my daughter (a widow)
George - her son
Victoria - her daughter

Ann and Patrick - friends of Simon and Jennie

Chapter 1

Pakistan

"Why did you bring Mother?"asked the unsympathetic official at a Pakistani airport as my son Simon struggled with my luggage.

"She comes," he said briefly and added, "Don't you look after your Mother?"

"I leave her at home, she is better there."

"How do you know?" asked Simon crossly.

The man looked puzzled, this is a man's world and Mothers stayed at home, they don't arrive at airports alone and hung about with bulky and misshapen packages. The official didn't answer Simon, perhaps it set him thinking for how did he know? I don't suppose he'd ever asked. We passed on and left him thinking, or so I hoped, for women are very definitely second class citizens here.

"She comes," Simon had said, but I was not at all put out, nor did I worry about his shouldering the heaviest of my baggage. Most of this had been requested. This is a Muslim country where Christmas is not celebrated and Christmas presents comprised the major proportion of the load. Also there were things that the family had left behind on their last trip home and bits for the computer which was invariably going wrong.

"She comes," had been Simon's answer years ago in Africa when he had turned on some newly made friends who were issuing an invitation to stay.

"Don't ask her, don't ask her," he implored them.

"Why ever not?" was the surprised reply.

"She comes," he said gloomily. I was hurt by this reply in those early days being under the impression that I was always welcome but I seem to have my uses and now it is "... when you come could you bring ...?" which passes for an invitation.

I had started out on this visit to my family in a slightly more extravagant frame of mind, quite different from my usual penny pinching procedure. I'd had another small windfall and decided to take a taxi to the airport. The taxi driver was a cheerful chap who did a regular Heathrow run and wasn't all that expensive. My grand-daughter Vicky, now at University, met me at the airport and we had a snack together before I boarded. That is - I had a snack, Vicky didn't appear to have eaten for weeks.

So here I was in Pakistan again, hopefully to be welcomed by Jennie (Simon's wife) and their children Elizabeth, Adam and Peter.

There are always plenty of visits planned for my arrival.

"You haven't been to Taxila yet," - "We might do Takht-e-Bahi at the weekend" or "You'll love the Swat valley."

I do love and look forward to all these places, the archaeological sites and the mountain scenery but I sometimes wonder when Simon will begin to notice and acknowledge my limitations. Increasing years make me admit that I am not so willing to climb K2 as I once might have been.

We still had some way to go before joining the family in the North West Frontier Province. It was early in the morning and we visited some friends nearby in the town of Islamabad. This was an Australian family where we were welcomed, served with coffee by a bowing servant and provided with facilities. Simon's friends seem to show no surprise at this Mother dumping at short notice, always I am given a friendly reception, it is so kind and greatly appreciated.

The drive north was a long one, Simon had his English speaking driver with him, that is Simon said he was English speaking and appeared to understand him as there was a good deal of laughter. I merely nodded and smiled as I had to admit I didn't understand a word he said.

We arrived to be greeted by my daughter-in-law, Jennie, and hurried to the school where the school play was about to be performed.

At this stage I had better re-introduce Jennie and my grandchildren, known already to those of you who have read my earlier book *And Mother Came Too*. Liz has grown, as children do, into a ravishing teenager. Adam, who is twelve, grows slowly and has a methodical brain. Peter, now nine, is a scatterbrain, they all have bright red hair. Needless to say I love them dearly, this includes Jennie, the one that didn't get away, the one I couldn't and didn't lose in those early days of Simon's passing girlfriends and fancies.

Jennie had been writing to me with advice.

"Wrap up," she said to me, "It's in a Tent."

A tent! My idea of a tent is a small canvas camping shelter and the vast, Arabian style colourful circus sized canopy in which the play was held so surprised me that I hardly noticed the play other than to make sure I could identify our own. A pity, for I'm sure it was good, but it was cold and I was tired. That night I slept well and dreamed of tents and deserts and aeroplanes.

It was great to wake up in this Northern town of Peshawar again, I'd been here before with Simon visiting our friends Ann and Patrick. My bedroom then had a view of the Khyber Pass and I thought this one of the highlights of my travelling career.

That morning Jennie had news for me.

"There's a Khyber Pass train going up on the Friday before Christmas," she informed me, "Would you like to go?"

Would I? Before it had merely been a glimpse into the far hills, now I was to experience the chugging uphill climb.

The house the family were living in was another marble palace, or so it seemed to me after the thatched beamed cosiness of our own cottage. Fortunately Jennie had housed me on the ground floor and I didn't have to climb the cold impressive stairway, the room was 'en-suite' so I had everything I needed.

Then I discovered the balcony and I realised its possibilities. Simon and Jennie share my love of plants and Simon, seeing me standing there in this deserted and overlooked area, started to visualise it with fencing and plants just as I was doing. The trouble with these large houses in Pakistan is that they are too close together. Even in our own small island houses of this size back home would have some ground and we should not be nearly holding hands with our neighbours. Not that there seemed to be any neighbours on the side where only a short passage divided us. I could have shaken hands if there had been anyone there, but it appeared to be empty.

"There are plenty of garden centres," said Simon, waving to a passing lady opposite, who rushed indoors worried by this male intruder.

Simon sighed and continued, "We have to find a Christmas tree of sorts, all the garden centres are grouped together, we'll all go, it'll be fun."

It was, and we also collected some fencing. I was to have my own garden room. "Almost as good as being in Purdah," I told Simon brightly. He didn't deign to reply.

We all wanted something different at the garden centre, I should say centres as we wandered from one to the other. This idea of grouping every similar merchandise together is typical of Pakistan, so shoe shops or material shops or jewellers are concentrated in one part, this saves a good deal of legging it about if, say dress material is the object. Here, in the plant section, there were plenty of adjoining garden centres.

We all agreed on a plant resembling a Christmas tree.

"It's a bit spiky," said Adam doubtfully.

"It'll look fine when hung about with all our decorations and things," said Peter.

"What things?" I asked with remembrance of all the baubles packed in boxes in my loft.

The children looked at me with looks of deep disapproval.

Should I, I asked myself, have brought these with me?

"The market is full of things that will do for decorations," said Jennie cheerfully, visualising another outing there in the old town with its colourful overcrowded streets. We all cheered up at that and continued in our quest for balcony plants, everything was so cheap compared to garden centre prices back home.

"I'd better get the truck," said Simon, viewing our collection with some misgiving.

To visit the old town we collected a small party of friends and we all set off for the wonderful market. Bazaar would be a better word for it as this has an oriental sound more suited to this medley of alleys and narrow streets with buildings nearly meeting overhead and hangings of all sorts suspended above.

Bazaars should be like this, crowded, colourful and enticingly full of exciting things to buy and at such tempting prices.

"I don't really need it," said Elizabeth for the umpteenth time as she pounced upon some trinket or other, "But it's so cheap."

'Oh reason not the need,' I quoted as I too battled with myself.

When Elizabeth stopped we all stopped and surrounded her as she attracted too much attention from the young men. I felt a grandmotherly scowl or two was necessary to show that she was well chaperoned and definitely not 'available'. We always had a crowd of interested admirers which made our progress difficult. We assumed they were admirers but even if not they appeared interested.

We hung ourselves about with garlands, tinsel, wedding trinkets and baubles, enough even to satisfy young Peter.

Simon did not accompany us on this frivolous shopping expedition, his eyes are generally fixed on more serious wares such as unsuitable furniture or large wall hangings, unsuitable as we have low beamed cottages at home and he will not always be housed in a high ceilinged mansion.

Last year, when visiting Ann and Patrick, Simon and I had been shown over this fascinating market and had been told that the Queen also came here. Perhaps it was spruced up for her, I'm sure she was kept clear of beggars and not shown any squalor.

The next day, Friday, was the day for the Khyber Pass train. I could hardly believe my luck when I heard that this train took passengers. Someone back home had assured me that it was military only and no foreigners were allowed on it. I wrote to a Travel magazine to tell them of this. It was printed under the heading 'Pleasure in Pakistan'. Perhaps the editor thought that pleasure was rare in Pakistan.

I wrote:-

'An exciting excursion in Pakistan is on the Khyber Pass train. This leaves Peshawar irregularly and I was lucky enough to obtain a seat on it just before Christmas. The train chugs up the winding track through rugged country towards the mountain pass. It stops for refreshments which are plentiful and included in the fare. These are laid out on tables at a station platform half-way through the journey. Armed guards travel with the train. Although somewhat spartan (it is as well to take a cushion and a blanket) it is an exhilarating experience.'

There was a bit in the local paper here and although the meaning is not quite clear I am reproducing it for interested readers.

'The decades old Landikotal railway line is still tourist attraction. The line was reopened in 1994 and until now 3000 enjoyed journey on it?'

Perhaps 'now' 3000 more will once more 'journey on it'.

There were no problems but I was glad of the cushion and blanket so thoughtfully supplied by Jennie. No-one looked at our tickets at the station, it was very early and the blanket was particularly welcome. The seats were hard so the cushion, too, came into its own. The armed guards were the usual handsome rugged men.

There are two great engines, one at the front and one at the back, it is a long pull up with thirty-four tunnels and countless bridges. Adam did count them and assured me that there were ninety-two as, indeed, the book said. What a feat this must have been to build such a railway, it was built by the British in 1920 - they would have been subduing someone. It is such desolate looking, barren countryside I'm surprised that anyone would want to fight over it, about it, or even in it.

This train was obviously a fairly new tourist attraction, too new to be much advertised. There was welcome all the way, even written on the train; at the stations people came out to look at us. I wondered where they had come from as the countryside did not look overpopulated.

Perhaps the noisy screech of the whistle could be heard and brought people out, this and the cow catcher on the front was enough to keep children and animals off the unprotected line.

The journey ended at Landikotal, children gathered here to stare and we stared back and on into the distance, there were rugged mountains on either side and the railway lines stretched before us into Afghanistan. There was a war on here of which we had heard horrifying tales. We had also seen the vast refugee camps, until I'd seen this I had no idea of the enormity of the problem. We seemed to be in a vacuum here, on a train marked 'Welcome to our Distinguished Guests' and just over there ...

Elizabeth broke into my thoughts. "There's supposed to be a lot of drug trafficking here at the border," she told me, proudly airing her knowledge.

"How do you know?" I asked, it all looked pretty innocent to me and she couldn't really know could she?

"Someone told me," she replied, "Perhaps not here, perhaps over there." She pointed vaguely in the direction of remote dusty hills. I agreed that anything could happen 'over there' but I wouldn't know what to look for and no-one approached me.

We were called back to the awaiting train, we returned downhill and progress was easier. Was everyone carrying drugs? I'll never know.

Simon now thought of his Christmas shopping, unable to resist his suggestion that I accompany him, I did so. He was anxious to find an out of town copper and brass workshop where he had heard that the goods were remarkably cheap. I find shopping with Simon somewhat worrying, he can so easily be carried away. We found this place, it was fascinating with totally unsafe working conditions and a delightful shop full of splendid wares, some very beautiful, some not, but all of interest especially to Simon. His mind was set on an exotic cooking pot, I also saw his eyes wander onto a magnificent Arabian Nights masterpiece for which, I could see, he had mentally found a resting place.

"It looks fine here," I said, "but back home - in the cottage ..." my words faded away as I visualised one more ornament in an already overcrowded sitting room.

"Perhaps you're right," he replied reluctantly, but brightening added, "We can come again before you go back and shop for presents."

All the way home he explained the workings of the cooking pot which I had on my knee and which he looked at lovingly every now and again. I hardly listened, it was complicated and I was sure I wouldn't have to use it.

"We'll 'do' Takht-e-Bahi tomorrow," said Simon. These are the ruins of a Buddhist Monastery and about fifty kilometres from us. "Are those the only shoes you've got?" he continued, looking at my easy-to-slip-off-in-an-aeroplane comfortable moccasins. They were, for shoes are heavy in luggage especially, as I pointed out, if you are loaded up with Christmas presents and 'could-you-bring' things.

Simon ignored this saying, "The going can be rough."

I knew this for the year before we had been to Moenjodaro.

"Perhaps someone can lend me a pair," I said, without much hope.

No-one had anything that would fit, the best being a pair of Adam's cast-off trainers.

Well! Why not?

"I'll get some trainers," I told my audience intrigued at the sight of Grandma in Adam's old shoes.

"Good idea," they all chorused seeing another shopping trip coming up. So Jennie took me to the Shoe Shop area where we found cheap copies of trainers with very expensive trademarks. It was pouring with rain and streets were thick with mud. There were six or seven assistants in a very small shop, all men of course. I am vague as to the number because there was a roof area which housed the shoes as well as some men. Verbal communication and boxes of shoes journeyed through a hole in the ceiling. I sat fascinated by this procedure, especially as these stocks never seemed to be dropped. Was there, I wondered, a training session for box throwing?

While I was stomping about in a pair of thick soled trainers, I noticed some Pakistani ladies trying on the daintiest of flimsy footwear, clad in brightly decorated useless draperies, they were watching me. I thought it was with horror but as I stepped outside to the broken pavements, muddy puddles and overflowing gutters, I wondered if it could be envy.

I was glad I made the effort, with a good deal of pushing and pulling, to climb up to Takht-e-Bahi. What a wonderful place to build a monastery; it was worth the struggle up not only because of the ruins but for the sake of the spectacular views from either side. On one side can be seen the hills surrounding the Swat valley and, on the other, the plains of Peshewar. Simon had already promised me a visit to the Swat valley after Christmas and the sight of these hills whetted my appetite. Not that I intended to do much climbing there but I had heard much of the beauty and productivity of the valley.

These ruins at Takht-e-Bahi give a remarkably good idea of the life of a Buddhist monk, parts are very well preserved, there are the monk cells, the kitchens and the refectory. So much has crumbled away, of course, and the decorations have all gone, but it is still impressive, as are the many stupas some of them still domed. These stupas are shrines and were built at different times by different visitors, pilgrims to the monastery.

I must again make it quite clear that this is not a guide book, these are my own impressions and the excellent travel books will tell you all you wish to know.

Some people don't like wandering about among ruins, perhaps they are sad places but I enjoy the chance for quiet meditation at a place like this. It was very peaceful.

We had brought our own lunch and had time to enjoy the peace and wander around at our leisure. We managed to lose each other as each of us had a different idea of ruin viewing. I found Adam in Buddha like pose sitting in a convenient niche, Simon gazing at a stupa under the impression that it was a storage place for grain and Jennie down in the dungeons or could it be a wine cellar? Elizabeth and Peter were quietly sitting on a stone while a small admiring crowd gathered, as Peter's hair was rather long I think the young men were under the impression that he was another girl. He is rather beautiful in an English sort of way. The crowd dispersed when a grumpy grandma appeared, these young men are always anxious to try out their English, preferably on someone young and attractive. We usually do have a following on these outings, the bright hair of the children and the determined grandma make us a conspicuous group. Not conspicuous as to our clothes compared to the Pakistani ladies who are hung about with gaudy unsuitable materials and much jewellery, everyone must think us very dull in our useful and comfortable clothes.

I saw Simon talking to one of our followers, was this man questioning the wisdom of bringing Mother into these hills. I heard Simon say "My Mother wishes to see these places." Did he mentally add, "And see them she is going to." He's a great one for Mother's sights is Simon, and as he pointed out going back, "It's all downhill, Mother."

Back at the villa we were all enthusiastic about my garden room, chairs were found and the fence went up. I had some difficulty in getting the many plants arranged to my satisfaction as the gardener (called a Mali) preferred straight rows and did not appreciate my (as I thought) artistic grouping. I'd regroup when I went up but often found them back in regimental lines. I had the feeling that he came in especially to do this as there was very little garden.

The room wasn't as peaceful as I had anticipated for the family and their usual assortment of friends now found it exactly right for their various activities, sewing, having meals, writing, playing ball and just sitting. Tea would be brought of course and a party atmosphere prevailed. In spite of this I found it a great place to relax and enjoy the plants, the names of some still a mystery to me.

"What's that one with the pointed leaves?" I asked Simon.
"I expected you to tell me," he replied unhelpfully.

"Oh, that's Cannabis," Liz assured us.

"It isn't labelled," I said doubtfully.

"Better not to know," said Simon.

The sun came out, school broke up and I settled down to enjoy my first Christmas in an Islamic country

Chapter 2

The Swat Valley and a wedding

I woke early on Christmas Day, made myself some tea and
retired again to bed happy in the belief that everyone had
been given the day off and the family were expecting to
have a lie-in until the time came for the opening of presents.

There was a great knocking at the door, it came again
and I thought the time had come to investigate. The boys'
room was on the same floor and I could hear voices and
activity so, hastily donning a dressing gown, I sent Adam to
find the cause of the disturbance.

"It's a deputation," said Adam, returning.

"What sort of a deputation?" I asked.

"All the men, it's a present giving deputation."

"Go up to your Father quickly," I told him as I hastily
retreated in order to scramble into clothes suitable for meeting
a deputation of Pakistani men.

I could hear the bustle and consternation from upstairs, Adam returned with a broad grin, delighted at having disturbed everybody and even Elizabeth could be heard asking what the fuss was about.

Simon arrived downstairs, he, Adam and Peter let in the 'deputation', this consisted of men who looked after the house as well as men who worked with Simon on the project. They all bore cakes and garlands.

Jennie and Elizabeth now arrived and we were all garlanded and presented with cakes. Cake giving is a Pakistani custom and we received many that day, some very ornate and much too sweet for my taste. There is a saying - "It's the thought that counts" and we were glad that these men recognised our special day for they were all Muslims.

The men departed having admired us and our decorations, tea having been served and our photos taken. Of course no drink was offered as Muslims are strict teetotallers.

I have my garland still but the cakes disappeared surprisingly quickly.

After present opening the rest of the day was spent trying out the oriental cooking pot and visiting other garlanded and cake rich friends.

The men who looked after us were, as far as I could gather, from the same family, it is normal here to recommend a relative, so our Chokidar or guard had brought along his nephew, a beautiful young man who wished to learn to cook. I doubt if he ever fulfilled his ambition but he was a pleasant soft-footed man who ironed my face flannel every day, I never discovered why.

The practice of using only one family had its advantages for if one was away another filled his place. Perhaps it was thought that we shouldn't notice the difference but Simon merely sighed and let it pass, as we knew perfectly well, of course.

I've mentioned the Mali with whom I raged a constant battle and whose duties were nominal as there was little or no garden. He did water the plants however, and as he had the use of a hosepipe was able to get his own back on his enemies if they passed by on the road. On Christmas Day, garlanded and clutching cakes, I forgave them all.

The Chokidar always tactfully disappeared if I joined the boys in any sort of game on the front almost-a-lawn. Perhaps I showed too much leg. I once asked him how many children he had.

"Six," he replied.

"How many go to school?" I now asked.

"Three go to school," he answered proudly.

"Are the others too young?"

"No, they are girls."

I withdrew, my quarrel was not with him.

My birthday falls just after Christmas and the visit to the Swat Valley was to be my birthday present.

It is indeed beautiful and so was the ride up, with the hills almost blue in the distance, then the flowing river with the terraced green hillsides with very varied dwellings and the productive, wide valley. The hills rising above were now, as it was winter, topped with snow. Perhaps this made it even more beautiful though my daughter, Amanda, visiting the summer before made me long to come and see for myself when she described the colours and the blossom. She was able to go to places we could not attempt in the snow - certainly not with a beginning-to-show-her-age Mother.

The guest house where Simon had booked looked down into the valley, it was a wonderful position. Booking was a luxury as there appeared to be no other guests, it was very cold. I suppose it was hardly the fault of the establishment, they were more used to summer visitors and skiers went even further up. Sadly all the time I was there I never seemed to get warm - alas for the ageing process. I'd brought my hot water bottle but filled with cold water it wasn't much good. There was a fire in the dining room and I moved as close to it as I could get and ordered tea. In this country tea is something understood and it's always hot.

"We'll go for a good warming walk tomorrow," said Simon bracingly. I will say this for my son, he won't let me indulge in a rocking chair mental state. The children of a friend of mine wrote her off when she reached sixty, "You've had a good life, now take it easy," they told her.

Not Simon.

"Put your skates on Mother" is more his line, or "It's not far to the top". Even "a good stiff walk is what you need". Jenny and the gang follow his lead though I sometimes feel that they think my rugger or tennis is not up to scratch. All turn a very blind eye if I falter.

I went into the small town at a fairly brisk trot and made friends with a young man with a gift shop. While I admired his goods he was anxious to talk about life in England. I asked him about his family as he was enjoying talking English and he said his Mother was old fashioned enough to wear the 'burkha' but his sisters were scornful of such a garment. I promised to return next day, which was my birthday, he asked where we were staying and was an early visitor next morning. He appeared at breakfast bearing a garnet incrusted rock.

"Your birth stone," he informed me. We promised to visit his shop after breakfast. I was greatly impressed by the young man's thoughtfulness but Adam cynically pointed out that it was an investment as we would be bound to visit his shop and spend more money. We did, of course.

I was ready for anything. I'd spend a better night than I'd expected as I had the good sense to take my hot water bottle to the kitchen for a fill up. The water in the bathroom was still cold but who needs to wash anyway, at this height the water only freezes on the body.

We started on the good warming 'it's-not-far-to-the-top' walk, Simon and Jennie are great walkers, the sight of an inaccessible (to me) mountain seems to stir their blood and act as a stimulus, they can't wait to get up it, they are not mountaineers, however and generally stop at the snow line. I wasn't sure where this was and I trudged hopefully in their wake. Liz, Adam and Peter also follow dutifully, I am amazed at their fortitude and think what strong legs they will have.

"It's all downhill," said Simon. It was, it was downhill to a crazy rickety bridge, then it went up again. I stopped at the snowline. Looking back beyond the bridge I could see the beautifully balanced guest house, looking very inviting.

I was willing to believe that the further we went, the more beautiful it became but the thought of the comparative warmth of that attractive building snugly tucked into the hill and the possibility of hot tea made me decide to investigate the region's geology. With a certain amount of disbelief in my preferring more academic pursuits they left me to my own devices. Several people asked me if they could help me as I went down, I had forgotten that lone women were an unusual sight.

A rhyme came into my head, I must have heard it in my youth written, I think, by Edward Lear.

"Who or why, which or what
Is the Akund of Swat?"

Yes, indeed, who was he? One thing is certain, I had never expected to want to know or to actually be there to find out.

Later that day our young shop friend again visited us, we had expressed interest in furniture and he now took us to visit all his uncles and other numerous relatives who appeared to be in the business. We went to a wonderful cellar, full to the brim with amazing pieces, he wouldn't let us buy here which was just as well, we could see Simon filling imaginary palaces, perhaps that is where it had come from. Another warehouse was also stacked high with old doors and other strange furniture, all beautifully carved wood. I contented myself with a foot square 4 inch high stool and we hurried Simon out, those wonderful doors would not do in our village, not to mention the trouble and cost of getting them home. I had read about all the things to buy in this area such as rugs, jewellery and precious stones but I did not know about this extraordinary and beautiful carved furniture. Perhaps not very portable for the normal tourist.

"Your tea shall come early," they told me in the kitchen when I went to fill my hot water bottle.

Their idea of early and mine differed although it did eventually arrive and tasted of washing-up liquid. Pleased as I was to think of the cleanliness involved I thought longingly of the custom in most hotels these days of a kettle and a DIY kit. How often have I deplored this system but I now saw its advantage much as I always enjoy the ceremony of the arrival of the tea tray brought, as always in this country, by unbelievably handsome men.

"We'll go for a drive," said Simon when we'd all assembled in the dining room and eaten well. He collected me firmly from my place beside the fire but, seeing the remains of my scrambled eggs, decided to have some himself. We eventually set off up the mountainside, it was a fantastic drive, the road was narrow, icy, steep and tortuous, it got worse, fortunately nothing came towards us.

"Perhaps I'd better turn round and go back," said Simon, hopefully I thought, as I could see no possible place for this manoeuvre.

"I think I'll get out and walk," said Adam.

"We all could," I said, "but it wouldn't compensate for the loss of 'Dad'."

"Better to have some weight in the back," said Simon cheerfully.

We all closed our eyes while hoping that Simon kept his open.

I suppose the view was compensation enough for our temporary panic as we looked down over the edge to the valley below, it was so beautiful, perhaps living by the sea makes such a contrast to this dramatic scenery. I love the sea, it's always interesting, but flat.

I want to visit this beautiful place again but in the summer, when it is hot in the plains, then it must be a wonderful experience to come to this cool, breathtaking valley. Also the road wouldn't be icy.

I could envy the Akund of Swat, whoever he was.

On the way home we stopped at Churchill's Picket. Churchill, as a young man, had served in the army here and it was said that he nearly lost his life on this hill. The picket on Damkot Hill is built on the ruins of very old fortifications, it is a great strategic point for there is an amazing panoramic view into the surrounding mountains and all the mountain passes can be seen. Now peacefully, tourists can enjoy what was a military necessity for many years, far back beyond the days of Churchill.

I didn't quite reach the top, it looked a little unsubstantial to me, but perhaps it is I who are no longer so substantial, the others offered to pull me but I declined as gracefully as

I could, I still had an excellent view which I enjoyed as the others climbed the last few dangerous looking steps.

Term started soon after our return, Simon disappeared to the University and Jennie had some hours teaching at an unusual school where most of the teachers appeared to be still on vacation.

I retired to the balcony which had taken on a floral room appearance. The sun shone.

A cart laden with oranges and pushed by a sad looking youth went by. I thought he ought to be in school, I called out to him and he wheeled his cart to the gate. I shouted down to our young man to buy me some oranges. I decided to make marmalade. It was a useful occupation, slicing up orange peel, I cut it up beautifully thinly and left it in soak. Jennie and I had promised ourselves a shopping expedition into the old town, I had back-home-presents to consider. If I said to Jennie "Let's go shopping," it didn't necessarily mean that I was going to buy anything. It's a form of entertainment to me much more exhilarating than watching 'soaps'.

Bartering is part of the process of buying out here, for the buyer and seller alike it's important for its social contacts as much as for the exchange of money and goods. How disappointing if the buyer, having been told the price, pays over the thirty rupees (or whatever). How dull must shopping appear in a country such as ours. Buying only begins with a suggested price, then the real stuff starts, the shake of the head, the suggestion of family ruination, the turn away, the return and when the tea appears serious bargaining starts.

When I'm told that - 'You are our Mother, we would never cheat you,' I know that I am approaching an acceptable price, either that or else their consciences are pricking them and they are trying to console me for the fact that I am about to pay for beyond the proper value. But friends have been made, definitely not enemies for there is always that possibility of your return. It is a very civilised affair, others have gathered, some family perhaps or friends and neighbours learning the technique.

When we returned from this expedition it was to find that the young man who ironed my face flannel so meticulously had thrown away my marmalade-to-be in the form of soaking orange peel. Perhaps he didn't understand the making of marmalade, or perhaps he thought he was doing me a good turn. I abandoned the project, in future we should eat our oranges uncooked.

Next door but one, beyond the empty house, was an enormous residence said to be inhabited by a millionaire. Long faces were pulled when he was mentioned, doubt being cast about the source of his wealth. I was intrigued, it must be shady, drugs perhaps. There was a great contrast between his ostentatious living and the beggars who congregated outside his gate on a Friday. Friday, being a holy day here, is the day for the giving and receiving of alms. I did wonder if I could don the Burkha and join the beggars. I've mentioned the Burkha before, it's the all enveloping garment with only a slit for the eyes worn by some women. Covered thus no-one could have known who was behind the mask and it is rude to stare. It would have been interesting to know what he gave, did he throw coins or notes? The coins are of little value. By my standards I am always hard-up but by the standards of the poor, in the many countries I have visited, I am classed among the rich. I did not go but it would have been an unusual experience to gaze without being seen at this notorious millionaire.

In the empty house next door we were surprised to hear and see great activity. Rumour soon reached us that it had been taken by the millionaire to house lady guests for a coming wedding for this was the wedding season. I've written elsewhere about this (see *And Mother Came Too*) and the various tents that mushroom in the towns, but this was something out of the ordinary. This was really flashy. We never discovered if it was a son or a daughter who was getting married.

Small faces appeared on the next door balcony trying to peer through our fencing, so if we were interested in them it appeared it was mutual, we were equally fascinating.

Liz's bedroom overlooked the next door yard and on into the millionaire's grounds. The next few days were punctuated by her cry of, "Do come and look," which naturally I did. An enormous tent went up and the comings and goings were endless. Of equal interest to me were the domestic arrangements in the next door back yard where food in enormous cauldrons was being prepared probably for less important hangers-on. This watching was an irresistible pastime. Night-time was different, the noise was not conducive to sleep. After a time I gave up, after all I was in a country where such celebrations were part of the culture, I felt that the life of a millionaire was not representative of life in Pakistan but it was a wedding in which everyone seemed to be involved. So I listened and wondered.

On the third night we had fireworks and I have never seen such a display, it was magnificent and we all collected at Liz's viewpoint to enjoy the free spectacle. Later on that night there was an electricity failure. All was silent, I can't say I was sorry.

I suppose the wedding took place in the tent so we didn't see the ceremony but we did watch the departure of the happy couple. We waved from the balcony.

"Good Luck," I shouted.

"You'll need it," added Liz gloomily. We wondered if it had been an arranged marriage and they hadn't even a spot of alcohol to get them through.

I returned to the intriguing back-yard scene.

Our watching from Liz's bedroom had not passed unnoticed by the workers there, they often looked up to see if we were in our viewpoint. I wondered what they thought of us, to them we must have looked as inclosed as their own womenfolk.

Some of these ladies arrived, imported no doubt for the domestic side, I should imagine they were fairly low down on the social scale. No expense was spared here either and several washing machines were delivered. The women walked round them delicately and with some misgiving touched various knobs. Washing was put in and, as nothing happened, was taken out again, and traditional methods of pummelling on a board took place. Nobody had explained plumbing, perhaps no-one knew.

Amanda rang, Tom had been taken ill and was in hospital.

"I must go," I said.

A visit to the airline offices only produced shakes of the head, why then did our friend the travel agent who had booked us on the Khyber Pass Railway journey have no trouble and immediately obtained my ticket? I am still puzzled.

Tom seemed happily recovered when I reached home. This did not surprise me.

Chapter 3

Christmas with Amanda

"You'll be alright this time," I assured Tom the following year. He agreed reluctantly as I was only going to the Midlands to spend Christmas with Amanda, George and Vicky.

Amanda had said, "You never spend Christmas with us."

"You could come here," I'd replied as my vow never to spend Christmas alone with an anti-Christmas Tom didn't preclude others visiting us. This vow I'd made (see *And Mother Came Too*) many years ago as Tom's total disregard of the whole festival season seemed unreasonable and failed to amuse me. In front of witnesses I said "Never again", and I've kept to this vow. But he hadn't been well and I didn't like to leave him for too long so a few days with Amanda seemed the ideal solution.

"There are all sorts of things happening here," Amanda insisted. "George and Vicky want to see you as well as visiting their friends." George and Vicky were both at University, George already on post graduate studies.

"Okay," I said, knowing that I would be getting itchy feet in the New Year and had every intention, as soon as Tom was better, of going out to Islamabad where Simon and family were now living.

My friend Eleanor and her three boys were going to spend Christmas up North near the Scottish border and offered me a lift. Amanda was delighted, "Why don't they break their journey and stay the night, there's plenty of room" she said, adding, "They won't mind sleeping on the floor will they?" Nobody objected, and the invitation was accepted.

It was a what-happened-to-global-warming sort of winter, it seemed to be raining, snowing, sleeting and freezing all at once. Floods were a hazard at first and then snow but we did eventually arrive.

Amanda was not at home, plenty of room here means plenty of floor space, just help yourself. Well, why not? Amanda is a great believer in people getting on with their own lives, this applies to herself as well as to her guests.

Eleanor and the boys found all sorts of hopeful corners in which to spread themselves and I, too, generally look around for a corner for myself where (1) no-one will stand on me and (2) I have reasonable access to a bathroom. I opened one door and to my utter amazement there was a bedroom in immaculate order, even to neatly folded towels on the made up bed and, on a well polished chest of drawers, a vase of flowers. Could this be a bedroom arranged for an adored Mother? Had it happened at last? I decided it had.

"Help yourselves to space," I said to the others and I shut the door.

When I rose next morning to make myself a cup of tea the journey round the house was quite hazardous as bodies were scattered about on various floors, chairs and beds. One rather larger lump proved to be George on the sitting room settee, he had arrived in the night and finding his own room occupied and being of a philosophical nature had settled himself down under various covers to await morning explanations. I gave him a hug, asked if the prickles were a beard or merely stubble and passed by, he didn't deign to reply.

The family of children also rose early and, finding an enormous jigsaw started to reassemble it on the floor. George on rising, started to unpack all his dirty washing then took up the rest of the floor space, it spread into the kitchen and the utility room, he had been away some time and had apparently been living where there was no washing machine.

Christmas began to look interesting especially when weather forecasts were issuing further warnings of bad weather and snow was falling.

"Why don't you stay?" asked Amanda oblivious to the chaos around here. It didn't look as if Eleanor would have to be persuaded, circumstances made it impossible to proceed. The snow continued.

What a lot Tom misses, we all had legs and boots, snow and a wonderful Christmas.

Chapter 4

Pakistan again

It was well after Christmas when I set out once again to visit the family now living in Islamabad.

Eleanor drove me to the airport, it was a wet and trying journey, or do journeys become more trying with increasing age? The flight was delayed and we had plenty of time for cups of tea and coffee, Eleanor being reluctant to leave me. I was looking forward to a good meal once the flight had taken off. I was disappointed here as it was surprisingly poor, then the flight filled up at Manchester and I was very cramped, my neighbours both being of unusual girth.

I was tired when I arrived in the early dawn, it was the first time for years that I hadn't spent Christmas with them, I had all their presents and their post with me, it was Friday and a day off so they were all there to meet me.

The house in Islamabad had been occupied by friends and, when these friends returned home, Simon took over the house and servant. This was the house I had visited last year before driving north.

"You've kept the same man," I said when I saw Joseph bowing once more.

"His time is limited," replied Simon.

"Oh?" Inquiringly.

"In fact he's very much on borrowed time," he said firmly.

"Why?" I now asked.

Simon was cautious. "Just make sure all your money is locked away," he replied.

"Then why keep him at all?" I wanted to know, we all leave our things about and there were plenty of other applicants for the job.

"I suppose because he knows the place, he speaks reasonable English, he's not a bad cook and he works hard."

These reasons seemed sound enough, and after a week I began to feel I could tolerate a bit of dishonesty. I'd say 'Tea' and tea would appear. My every wish was anticipated. This devotion could pall after a time but for a short while it was refreshing. He was a hard worker, the place was kept clean, he was cheerful and even appeared to enjoy the work, I think I, too, would be reluctant to part with him but I should continue to lock up my money. I know he ate my sweets and he made funny noises which irritated the family but when I viewed a beautiful pile of newly ironed clothes I felt in a forgiving mood.

After I returned home Simon told me during a phone call that Joseph's time had indeed run out.

"Dishonesty is a bad habit," said Simon. "He started taking things and selling them, and when we were away the phone bill was enormous. I don't think he realized that the bill was itemized, so we knew they weren't our calls. I think he had a woman in too, not his wife, who lives a long way off, she helped herself to Jennie's things. We've a good couple in now, thoroughly honest."

So that was the end of Joseph.

He was here this trip and 'chuntering' around me, I took Simon's advice and locked everything away.

I went onto the balcony, there were a few plants there but the back yard was jam packed with greenery, all in neat rows.

"They came in a moving garden," explained Peter.

"It was a truck," said Adam, but I could still imagine the moving garden.

Simon appeared.

"Can I have some on the balcony?" I asked, "It looks rather bare up there."

He looked at the back yard - perhaps he hadn't noticed it before.

"If you ever see the Mali, get him to do it," he said.

"When does the Mali come?" I now asked.

"When the mood takes him, so try to catch him and get him to make it nice up there for you."

To catch him? Was he some sort of wild beast? I had seen a man in a green almost-a-turban, dashing round, perhaps he really did need to be caught. I watched him now in envious disbelief, these pot plants comprised the larger part of the garden. I thought of the long back-breaking days ahead of me at home, my lawn looking more like a field and many areas which I try to pretend I am purposely leaving to be environmentally friendly. There is so much labour out here, some good, some indifferent, but it is still there and young men often come to the door seeking employment.

I watched the green head rushing round checking up on the pots and brushing the pocket handkerchief piece of grass with an inadequate brush. He was quite willing to carry pots up and arrange some more straight rows, we continued to play the game of rearranging all the time of my visit for I prefer my own grouped arrangements, Pakistanis prefer plant regimentation.

Simon put up the rush screens known as chick, Jennie found some chairs and my holiday had begun. The weather was cold enough for an English Christmas, the sun which had inspired my roof garden now went in, it started to rain, the gas went very low and all the people going by were huddled into blankets, I had wondered why it seemed to be the main article of dress, now I knew and resolved to buy myself one at the first opportunity.

On my second day Simon's Urdu teacher arrived, he had arthritis but, while giving him my sympathy, I envied his ability to get every ounce of benefit from it. This made me think that I could do more for my own welfare, for he not only had the fire full on with a warm place beside it, he also had tea served immediately, cake or biscuits and the television on.

"Why?" I asked Simon, "I thought he was supposed to be teaching."

"He likes to watch the dancing girls," replied Simon.

"Surely he hardly needs them," I remarked hastily, "With everyone dancing around him."

"Maybe you're right," agreed Simon, who was beginning to tire of the palaver, "I'll put on the cricket instead, it'll be less distracting."

Simon's Urdu is improving, so I decided not to be too spiteful but I am determined to get the maximum attention and to make the most of any failing. Next year's air journey will be different, no struggling with luggage, no hunting for trolleys, no long weary walks to the plane while attractive little buggies go by. Next year I'm going to be on one. Thinking, as I so often do, of those wonderful Victorian lady travellers and determined not to be too soft, pride had

had the upper hand. No longer - forget pride and from now on ...

I liked this house though I'd have liked more garden. Islamabad is a well planned city and the town itself has wide streets and plenty of room but in these residential areas the houses are much too close together for my taste and sadly interspaced with rubbish dumps. Some owners make the most of their meager plots so that there are many attractive shrubs and trees. I greatly envied an orange tree growing down the road, our own miserable specimen didn't look like producing. I solved this problem by buying a bag of oranges from our little market across the road and tried to convince everyone that my green fingers had produced such fertility.

"My visa's run out," said Simon distractedly, a few days later, "I'd better go and investigate, my contract hasn't finished so a visa will only be a formality."

He was depressed when he returned.

"Some petty official, no help at all, just told me I had to leave the country," he informed us. We all looked at him and looked at our papers, mine were the only ones in order. I was horrified, would I be the only one left to sort things out.

It was Ramazan, the days are for fasting and for ill tempers, working days are short while everyone thinks of the night feasting, no doubt this official was tired and had thought of a quick way out.

"Don't worry," said Simon. "It'll take time but it will be okay in the end."

It was, thankfully, and we all breathed again.

We had an invitation to Peshawar for the following weekend as Ann and Patrick were leaving, they were giving a farewell party. We travelled up with another mutual friend, John, who had a largish van into which we could fit. The party was in full swing when we arrived with a great tent and carpets all over the lawns.

"This I must have photos of," I exclaimed as we climbed from the van. "I want all my friends to know that I go to the sort of party where there are carpets on the lawn." We rushed for our cameras.

A great charcoal fire burned too, the morning was still cold and guests were gathering round it, tables and chairs were scattered around, food and drink abounded. Inside was a different story, bare boards and packing cases with the last remnants of their life in Pakistan. Goodbyes can be sad but this was a cheerful affair, we knew we'd meet again, the sun came out and the food was wonderful.

Dusk came, most guests left but we stayed and cooked fried eggs on a shovel, Simon insisted on this, I can't think why, perhaps as a contrast to oriental luxury and to associate with humbler practices.

As Ann and Patrick were furnitureless, Ann had arranged for us to stay the night with some friends of theirs. John took us there, it was a large comfortless house and the occupants didn't appear to be there.

"They're all ill," explained John who had gone to explore, "they said to make ourselves at home down here, they may see us in the morning."

It was freezing cold so I filled my hot water bottle and appropriated the only bed I could find, the others made themselves comfortable on various bits of furniture or on the floor without complaint.

In the night I thought I heard them say, "The cat has been sick," but I decided to ignore it.

I never did meet the mysterious 'they' for we all woke early, breakfasted at a nearby cafe and departed after watching the dismantling of the party furniture, tent and carpets. The house now had a look of temporary chaos so different from its usual appearance of finished comfort for

Ann has no children and takes great pride in her house where everything always looks lovely.

We were to take Ann's wee doggy until she and Patrick were settled in their house in Nepal. Nepal? I'd never yet been there.

On our way home we saw a woman run over - perhaps killed, no-one stopped and no-one went to help her. We were all upset knowing there was nothing we could do and helpless with a feeling of futility. No-one will touch a woman, so what happened I've no idea.

"We can't stop either," said John. "We didn't see what happened and we might even be accused of doing it."

"I need tea," I said. "Can we stop somewhere?" This was a welcome suggestion and we drew up at an expensive hotel. Was this a necessary contrast to the sickening scene on the road?

All was calm here but somewhat flashy, we all sat quietly and drank our tea. How different are our cultures.

How different indeed and our use of the language -

Delicious fish dishes attract elite ### *by Rana Mubashir*

ISLAMABAD:

With the temperature of sister cities falling, the management of Pearl Continental goes for a week-long Sea Food Festival where western and local elite cluster over a rare taste of ocean fish dishes.

Dripping fresh delicacies exquisitely prepared king fish, smoked salmon, seafood are served at the Marco Polo.

A large crowd turned to have a taste of sea food, were attracted by the basic fish brawth specially made in a different variety of soaps.

From fishermen net to chef's skillful hands, lobsters, prawns and sole fish present a delicious outing.

On the display are squid fish, which is netted from the deep sea water, jumbo prawns, tiger prawns cooked with and without head and for tasteful people their is sniper fish.

Meat loaf fish, all seafood prawns salad, Mexican style fish and Italian and provincial style prawns are on display with green salads decorated around. The foreigners enjoying their meal Saturday night seemed a little bit bilked when their request for dancing on the tune of 'buzuki' was turned down.

Maintaining the Islamic traditions, the PC management did not serve choicest brews like champaign and beer, normally served with the sea food.

However, desserts like pudding, cheese cake, coffee cake, apricot smholina was enjoyed by the people dropping till late hours.

To maintain the standard and decorum, Maitre hotel, Solhal Aziz and chef Aslam Khan along with Newaz were remained on their toes, making sure that the outing becomes a memorable one.

I like this extract from the local paper. I like the idea of the riotous degenerate westerner demanding the dancing girls and the contrast with the clean living upright Pakistanis with their Islamic traditions. Were they unable to see the joke? The lemonade was obviously flowing freely.

"We'll go to Taxila tomorrow," said Simon arriving in late on Thursday night.

"Oh! good," said Jennie, "we can take lunch."

"Anyone else coming?" I asked.

It seemed that only Adam was 'free', the others had invitations out for the day. Times are changing in the family, it's no longer, "we're going," but "Who's coming?"

There is so much of Taxila it would probably take years to tour it thoroughly. Simon handed me Sir John Marshalls' book for Sir John had spent years on excavation there.

"We can't see it all," said Simon. "We'll do Jaulian and Sirkap, it'll give you a good idea of the place, maybe next year we can go again."

"How big is this Taxila?" I asked, "and what are Jaulian and Sirkap?"

"They're two of the cities there," he replied, "there are probably about fifty sites and the whole area is about ten miles by five, I think," he added.

We started early and went first to the museum, I was very impressed with this, there were excellent exhibits of art, coins and all sorts of domestic utensils which give an idea of day to day living, I love this as it makes these ancient sites so human. There were toys and jewellery here too and everything was so well looked after which I cannot always say for the various museums I have visited. Sites too are often ill maintained.

There's a great feeling about Taxila, it was built up over a period of about a thousand years from 500BC onwards, it was then called Sadad by the White Huns. I don't know a lot about the White Huns but it all sounded very modern except that the raiders were not carrying Kalashnikovs.

At Jaulian there was a Buddhist Stupa and a monastery, all very well preserved. We wandered around and again I came across Adam sitting Buddhist fashion in an alcove, I took his photo and thought how placid he looked there, a passing guide nearly mistook him for the real thing but returned and indicated that it wasn't encouraged.

There were plenty of people trying to sell 'genuine antiques'.

"All fakes," said Simon, "but buy them for George if you want to."

I'm always soft about these things but even fakes are copies of something. George is now a fully blown archaeologist, I wanted him to come with me but he had been ill so wherever I go I try to take back something for him such as news of the various sites and objects of interest to him, even if they are fakes.

We had our picnic at Jaulian and then drove on to Sirkap. In some of the photos we took I look older than the walls so well built and solid are they and with much decoration still in place. Walking down the now grassy roads it is possible to think of the shops and houses with the occasional Stupas. My diary says we were attacked by goats. I don't remember this or even why, I expect the goats kept the grass cropped, perhaps they fancied a change of diet.

I've said before that this isn't a travel book nor a book about archaeology, and in the case of Taxila Sir John's book will tell the dedicated all they need to know.

I shall go back one day, preferably with George.

Chapter 5

The Mosque

"You can all come to the mosque with my class if you like," said Peter.

We did like and Simon, Jennie and I joined the class outside this enormous mosque one Monday morning. When visiting Islamabad before with Simon I had only glimpsed inside, and admired the pale blue carpet and the chandelier.

Mosques are for men only, if the women want to pray I suppose they have to stay outside and on my earlier visit I had peered in and admired the chandelier and the carpet in a resentful sort of way. With the school organized party we were all admitted after leaving our shoes in the appointed place. This time while sitting on the pale blue carpet I re-admired the chandelier, a magnificent globe of light.

"Are there any questions?" asked our studious and seemingly devout guide, expecting, I think, religious issues.

"Yes," said Peter pointing worriedly to the chandelier. "How many bulbs are there and how do you change them?

The young man was not at all put out and we were all glad he knew the answers, such questions of a practical nature must have been considered in the construction programme. This is a strange tent construction with four space rocket-like minarets pointing to the heavens.

Everyone was offered the chance to go up a minaret but I declined, knowing my own limitations. Simon Jennie and Peter decided for it and although they came down considerably puffed out they said the view was worth it.

The serious young man now told us how his religion revered the elderly and especially mothers, Simon put his arm around me, Peter following suit put his around Jennie, sadly my thoughts turned to the many old beggars who accost me in the streets, was this lovely idea solely in the young man's mind or for the better well off.

Chapter 6

It's all downhill Mother!

Above Islamabad there lies a wonderful range of hills called the Margallas, I could see them clearly from the balcony tantalisingly near, with one or two jutting peaks and some rolling gentler slopes, green and wooded. They didn't look dark and forbidding at all as some of the ranges do, they looked well within my capabilities. I heard that a walk was being planned and I asked Jennie if she thought I could make it.

"Good news," she said when she had enquired as to the composition of the party.

"Someone has strained his knee, wants to go but wants to go at his own pace, it's an ill wind," she added.

Dennis was a determined Canadian who wasn't going to be put off by a hurting knee, we got on well, each pretending it was the other holding up the party.

We all set off in a rackety bus, up the winding road with its hairpin bends, dangerous corners and other equally unsuitable vehicles coming down or trying to pass.

Simon went his own way, preferring to take his own tough vehicle up and leave it in a place near the end of the walk. He departed with his usual cheerful, "It's all downhill, Mother." He joined us on our still upward rough track. Coming down I was surprised to see a moving haystack, it occupied the whole of the track and it wasn't until one of the party greeted it with, "Salaam Alaikum" that I realised it had legs. Was there a field up there and where did he keep his animals? Later we looked down into fertile gentle valleys and beyond the first ridge the hills stretched away into the distance, it was a greater range than I had imagined.

We walked on, the day was fine and the sun came out, the going became more rugged but Simon and Jennie urged me on, Dennis, too, stayed with me, the others had long since disappeared. The walk was only a day's outing, one could walk for weeks in these hills, perhaps visiting the quiet resting small farms.

I started to tire and with a "Wait Here" Simon rushed off, we plodded slowly on, yes it was downhill now and we heard the noise of a vehicle. Simon had managed somehow to urge his useful wagon up the track. Turning a corner we saw him approaching, I clambered wearily in but when we met the others they too were tired, so perhaps my school days of racing up and down the hockey field had paid off. It was exhilarating up there in the hills, compared with other Pakistani towns Islamabad is less polluted but it felt fresh and clean up there and worth the 'up' and the 'all downhill'.

There's something about hills, I may never return to the Karakorams, in the winter when I visit many places are inaccessible. Amanda managed to reach the Hunza valley because she went in the summer. Warned against the heat in the plains she wisely went North into the hills and visited places I shall never see. Years ago I read about the Hunza people who were supposed to be the healthiest on earth, what with living on their own produce and their long mountain walks they had perfect teeth as well as perfect health. I asked Amanda about this but she seemed doubtful.

"Why walk twenty or thirty miles when it's easier with wheels?" she answered with another question, and added, "Plenty of 'goodies' there now, things have been taken up and people have come down to view civilisation for themselves."

I wonder how their teeth are now?

I had returned from a shopping spree when I realised that there was an atmosphere and something was being kept from me.

"What is it?" I asked, "Something's up."

"Tom again, he's in hospital, best place, don't worry," said Simon.

An early flight again into a snow-bound bitter England.

How long can I continue to travel? Is there a God of travel? I hoped so and put up a small prayer.

Somewhere along the line I must have pleased the powers above for, as the gloomy winter days passed and signs of Spring appeared, this prayer was answered and Malcolm Fish came into our lives. Alas, no halo, but just an ordinary-do-anything, reliable, helpful man. We heaved sighs of relief as things returned to normal.

Chapter 7

Vicky's Impression of Egypt

Said Julius Caesar, "Let me have men about me that are fat."
I couldn't agree less, I admire the 'lean and hungry look'.
Fat people don't look like workers, perhaps Caesar wanted
his men hanging about where he could see them. I like
men to look as if they can rush around and do a little plotting
not with slow treading feet and overhanging bellies. If they
are not doing things at least looking as if they could. This
man had a lean, brown, muscular look about him.

"I've just started up my own business," said Malcolm Fish,
"someone suggested that I call on you." He produced his
references, this was more like Pakistan.

"What do you do?" I asked.

"Anything," he said, "I don't mind what I do, gardening, housework, odd jobs, - painting," he added, looking round our shabby walls.

"Weeding," I suggested, "feeding the cats if I was away, husband minding?"

"Fine," he said. He was on. We had a bearer, a cook (if needed) a mali all rolled into one with no complaints that it was somebody else's job. Added to that he was healthy and good looking (dare I say middle-aged?), surely an answer to prayer. That visit to the mosque wasn't wasted.

I'd said to him, "If I go away". It wasn't 'if', it was 'when' for Amanda and I were contemplating a Nile river trip. Neither of us had ever seen the wonders of Egypt and this seemed to us to be the best way to go about it although we were not keen on organised tours. I thought this trip would be a sounding out time to see if Tom liked Malcolm enough for me to set out on my usual longer trip to the family at Christmas. It takes Tom time to adapt, not only to new ideas but to new people. He'd looked with approval at Malcolm, I was hopeful. Tom too looked with distrustful eyes on the over indulgent look of the heavy corpulent. He had always been slight and energetic and he was suspicious of any unlike himself. He would never be one of those who liked a good fat wife who can show to the world how well he feeds her; in some African countries it is a sure way of showing wealth just as, in other countries, wives are hung with gold. Tom has never been an advocate for these methods, perhaps in a wealthy country such flamboyance is unnecessary. So, like me, he too thinks as I now repeat 'let me have men about me who are thin'. Such was Malcolm Fish.

The family were enthusiastic when I told them over the phone.

"Malcolm," said Liz, "that means a calm mali and Fish, he's bound to bring good weather," optimistic this perhaps.

"Malcolm is a man of peace," she continued. Liz is 'into' peace just now.

"He certainly is bringing peace of mind to me!" I replied.

It was much later in the summer when the family looked him over.

"He looks like a Red Indian," said Peter who was reading a book about North American pioneers.

"No feathers though," said Adam.

"He'd look great in feathers," said Peter.

"Or without," I muttered, "but he's my idea of Sherlock Holmes."

"Too healthy looking for Holmes," answered Adam, "Holmes was on drugs you know."

Drugs? Sherlock Holmes, my hero? It has a different sound these days.

But Malcolm came and was well settled in by the time of the summer holidays.

Shortly after his arrival Tom had managed to catch a bad cold which was followed by bronchitis, I was too anxious to leave him and my holiday place in Egypt was taken by Vicky. So it was from Amanda's and Vicky's account that I describe the trip. I was cheered by their tale for I had been so disappointed, after reading letters and hearing their story I decided that perhaps it was not for me.

"I reckon you had a narrow escape," said Vicky, "we were 'tombed out' for one thing." I think this expression meant that they saw too many tombs, it was a new one on me.

My father had lived in Alexandria for a time and his descriptions of the pyramids and the wonders of the Nile had awaked some response in me, a desire to see these for myself had stayed with me over the years.

"All this I must see," I told myself but that was then and not now and 'now' is probably one long touristy expedition.

A leaflet had come through the post advertising a trip down the Nile on an exciting boat with interesting sights on the river banks, seeing the fertility of the land and including visits to the temples, the sphinx and the pyramids possibly on camels ... I was enthralled, I was forgetting that my father's tales were pre-war.

Amanda had agreed to join me somewhat reluctantly, she wanted to see such sights but was dubious about the package deal. She had probably read less romantic fiction than I had, most of which she pointed out was in the travel brochures.

After the trip she wrote, "I wanted to see the sights but I can read and I didn't want a lot of unconnected chit-chat. I knew what I wanted to see and I loved the river, the boat was small (there was not room for a murder) but, compared to the environmentally unfriendly gin palaces, it wasn't too bad."

Vicky said that Amanda became increasingly antagonistic as time went on, the heat didn't help, nor the rigid regime.

"Neither of us liked being herded about in groups listening to bored guides telling a much repeated story nor were we interested in put-on shows," she said, "all the same our guide was better than most and made the trip better than it might have been, he was well dressed and passionate about his Egyptology. He was intelligent and had a good sense of humour and so made our tours around the temples bearable. If he saw interest flagging he would tell us a story, he was lively and well informed and when we saw some of the other guides relating information in bored monotone deadpan voices, we thanked our lucky stars."

"I think," said Amanda, "that they turn out graduates in Tourism and Egyptology from the Universities all destined to be guides on the big cruise ships, we kept meeting these other parties looking as bored as their guides."

I agreed that I did not wish to be herded about and perhaps I had not missed much. I may never see the pyramids. I persuaded Vicky to write me an account of her impressions and I reproduce it here.

Egypt by Vicky:

The package deal flight came as a shock and my feelings of misgiving progressed with the journey. I was used to amassing the usual collection of miniatures and here all drinks had to be paid for. Added to this the headphones were £2.50 for a loan of 5 hours, and I couldn't see the film provided for our entertainment. I settled down to look at our fellow passengers, they seemed to me to be all white haired, plump respectable tourists eagerly awaiting their 'holiday of a lifetime cruise down the Nile' with the latest in camera equipment around their necks, white sun hats and T-shirts at the ready and with enough pleasantries nervously exchanged with fellow tourists to irritate even the most tolerant and stoic traveller.

We arrived at Luxor airport and duly stood passively awaiting our luggage before making our way out. Before, when I have been travelling, I have always been slightly scornful of the people flocking into their groups and standing by their appropriate signs, I expect you've felt the same. This time we were those people and we gathered around the company rep who efficiently looked at our tickets and directed us to our bus. There didn't seem to be anyone of my own age among the passengers, they were all middle-aged and hung about with touristy paraphernalia. My heart sank.

We drove to the boat and I had my first glimpse of Egypt with flat fields and fertile looking reddish brown soil, unfamiliar crops with interesting looking ditches part of the complicated irrigation system that one associates with the Nile. I could identify date palms and there were other different palm species.

Why did you bring Mother?

Approaching the town we could see square buildings with flat roofs, streets with red dust and the scruffy look of many developing country towns with pot holes, crooked paving slabs and dust everywhere.

We arrived at the quayside and all along the quays as far as the eye could see were these huge cruise ships obscuring our view of the Nile lined up three or four thick and nose to nose.

I knew that Nile cruises were big business but it was still a shock and I felt a sickening feeling to see the evidence of this - all these huge ugly ships with their generators belching out smoke made me anxious about the effect on the environment. We must have driven about half a mile alongside these monstrosities before coming to our own boat which was small and looked dwarfed and dowdy looking compared with the ones we had been observing. It was all by itself, a fact which we were to be glad about at night time when crowds of party-goers returned to their ships shrieking with laughter and losing their way when they couldn't remember the location or name of their own vessel.

So we reached our own little boat, tired and travel weary and in need of rest and solitude, not a bit of it as we had our first taste of the regime (more of this later) and were herded into the lounge area and given a lecture on the culture of Egypt and of the joys in store for us. What a lecture, my mother's hackles were rising already at this patronising "English-package-tourists-are-a-bit-dim-and-always-getting-dehydrated-in-hot-climates-because-they-will-drink-alcohol-and-fall-asleep-sunbathing-and-therefore-need-talking-to-very-firmly" speech. Her hackles didn't go down again until a week later when we arrived safely home to my student flat. Except that the boat was a bit small it wasn't at all bad, the cabin was tiny, there were two levels of these with an open sun deck on top, we weren't very comfortable because we were so cramped, there were two minuscule hard bunks against the wall, a small bedside cabinet between and a dribbling shower and basin from which hot and cold water were sometimes available, as well as a fair amount of small talk from where we did not know. Luckily for us we then discovered you could hear every conversation emanating from the cabins below, to the sides and behind us before committing the unforgivable solecism of dissecting in detail the personality defects of all one's fellow travelling companions. This could have resulted in a nasty situation! We also discovered that the faint strains of a jazz tune we could hear wafting through the air was coming from the bedside cabinet. However much we fiddled with the knobs we could neither turn the sound up nor turn it off, it was disconcerting to hear this autonomous contraption which seemed to have a life of its own.

It has to be said when cruising along in our pretty little paddle steamer, sunshine, good book in hand, relaxed watching life on the Nile go past that life does not get a lot better than this, but I must now tell you about the regime in case you are fooled once more.

At 8 o'clock sharp the gong went for breakfast. If one didn't appear, then concerned waiters would be sent to knock on your door to make sure you weren't ill or simply slacking. Anyone not eating breakfast would receive a slapped wrist, because as we all know, breakfast is the most important meal of the day, and all tourists need to keep their strength up for the rigours of sightseeing.

At 9 o'clock sharp the gong would ring, and everyone should assemble for the day's sightseeing.

At 1 pm the gong would ring and everyone should assemble for lunch. Anyone not eating lunch would received a concerned visit from the waiters to see if there were any stomach problems or whether one was slacking. Any slackers received a slap on the wrist.

At 2 pm the gong would ring for the afternoon's sightseeing.

At 7 pm the gong would ring for dinner. Anyone not eating dinner would also receive a visit from concerned personages.

At 4 o'clock on the afternoons we were on the boat tea and biscuits were served on the sun deck.

Alcoholic beverages were available from the bar on request. Gorgeous Egyptian coffee was also available after much coaxing and persuasion that some of us undiscerning and stupid foreigners really did prefer local stuff to Nescafe!

As I suppose on most package holidays, our days were completely mapped out for us down to the last half hour. It was a truly marvellous experience seeing the temples and tombs, Karnak, Luxor, the valley of the kings, Abu Simbel and the rest. I think that the splendour, the beauty, the history of the temples, the awed feeling I got when I realised just how long these structures have survived, is the memory of Egypt which I will always remember.

However it was hot, sticky work and after the 12th explanation and run down on dates, history whose temple which pharaoh, how old, what the hieroglyphs mean, funny stories, the information stopped penetrating the brain. One of the temples sticks in my brain more that the others. This was on the Luxor's west bank, the Temple of Hatshepsut. The guidebook in a brief description said it was as if it had been built by nature itself and is one of the 'finest monuments of ancient Egypt'.

Call me a philistine if you must but for some reason I couldn't help thinking how well this temple would fit into post 1960's Birmingham. Perhaps its original appearance with its gardens, its trees and its sphinx-lined causeway would have been more spectacular.

My Mother took a particular liking to the Avenue of Sphinxes at Luxor temple, she said they bore a curiously striking resemblance to her father.

[This I wish I had seen - J.V.]

Yes, I think I must be a philistine, because for me, the high point of all the sightseeing was seeing the Aswan High Dam. I've heard so much about it and the complexities of human water use all the way down the Nile, that I was truly fascinated by this awesomely huge dam. One of the low points was seeing Abu Simbel, one of the most famous temples, out in the desert on the banks of Lake Nasser. We had to get up at 4am to see this marvel, to beat the heat and the crowds. By the time we got there I was not fit for anything much. True, the temple was pretty spectacular, but it was still much the same as all the other temples we had seen. It was saved from being flooded by Lake Nasser back in the 1960's in a huge rescue operation by UNESCO, and archaeological teams carved the structure up into blocks and moved it piece by piece. I'm glad it wasn't flooded, but somehow the thought of it being carved into blocks and transported detracted from the romance of the place. Ah well, maybe I was just tired and grouchy and hot that day.

One of the main problems with being on a package tour was that we were wrapped in cotton wool, and were not allowed to explore Egyptian culture firsthand, go off on our own around town (except for a ridiculously short hour long shopping trip we were allowed on the last day) in case something bad should happen to us and we blamed the tour company. I didn't really get a glimpse into the culture of real Egyptians. Going round the markets was very funny sometimes, because everywhere we went my Mother was asked how many camels she would accept for her daughter! when figures got into the thousands, she started to look quite interested, until the practicalities of how to transport them to England, and what one would do with them in the first place ticked over in her mind. Phew!

[I must add here that Vicky is a very attractive young woman - J.V.]

Egyptians are very very tricky bargainers. I do believe that I am quite a good bargainer myself from spending three weeks by myself in Bali's notorious Kuta with white skin indicating wealth, but very little money to my name. Tourism has started to corrupt the gentle Indonesian normal bargaining practices in some places, but in general it is fair, and when a price has been fixed everyone is happy. In Egypt, I was first of all taken aback by the prices of souvenirs - not many bargains to be had there, still a little cheaper than buying from the old Oxfam catalogue but not much. Secondly, I was looking out for a hanging throw type affair with colourful geometrical Muslim patterns on it. The shopkeeper said to me in encouragement 'very cheap, very cheap, come in come in' and he mentioned a price which was indeed very cheap and within my price range. So we entered into his shop, and knowing that I would in all probability buy something, accepted his offer of refreshments. Then came the time for bargaining over the hanging, so I mentioned the price he had told me outside. "Don't be silly," said he "did you really think anything that beautiful could be that price? I was only telling you that to get you into my shop in the first place to stop you going to my rival down the road instead!" Well, that's no bargaining technique I know. We walked out in disgust, much to his chagrin.

I really don't know whether it was the fact that we were cotton-wooled by the package company, or whether other people have had similar experiences, but I really do feel that everyone was out to trick us out of our money. On several occasions one of our group would be stopped by the picturesque sight of a lone Egyptian child playing with a dog, a donkey or some other cute domestic animal. They would stop for a photo opportunity ... and as soon as they had taken the photo, up would pop the child's mother from behind the wall and ask for a cash donation.

Two friends found that entering a market they were greeted with much friendliness but on returning empty handed the atmosphere changed, was ever threatening and the girl was called a whore.

In general the people were friendly and proud of their heritage, with sunshine and the Nile they had everything they could want. Our guide had this enormous sense of national pride, his country had everything, his people were part of one of the grandest civilisations in history whilst ours were probably still running after the woolly mammoth, perhaps this explains his air of patronising benevolence towards us.

I felt disbelief at the sight of a whole economy thriving off package tours and the strangeness of being one of thousands of package tourists, all doing exactly the same thing according to their itineraries, it was quite scary for me feeling, as I did, like one in a flock of sheep. Tourists were definitely seen more as mealtickets than people though, and this was slightly disturbing. Maybe I am too used to the gentle Indonesians, who are on the whole contented to watch life go by, and tourists are as much a source of entertainment as cash with their funny shapes and sizes and customs.

Amanda and Vicky were right, this would not have done for me any more than it did for them, I had the impression that they were glad to be home. It was, I had to admit, very different from my father's time. He, too, would have hated it. For myself I like to see more of places I visit other than the put on shows for tourists. I like to see something of the domesticity of the people in the country around me. Maybe I miss a lot but I think I gain more. I try to travel inexpensively and I unscrupulously scrounge on my friends. No longer do any of us like being herded around listening to bored guides telling their much repeated stories. We're not package tour people, we prefer to do our own thing, if disasters occur it's our own fault but we learn by our mistakes, one mistake is to go on a package tour.

Simon rang to enquire after his father's health.

"Glad he's better," he said heartily, "it's getting very hot here, it's fine where I am in the hills but it's too hot for the children, they break up next week, shall I send them home?" His voice had a positive tone to it.

"By themselves?" I asked, well why not? We are a travelling family and unaccompanied minors are well looked after these days. Not that they need it, Elizabeth and Adam are very competent and won't lose young Peter.

So I agreed and looked forward to the visit which was probably already booked anyway.

Tom was less than enthusiastic and his face when I told him did not reflect my own happy countenance, the prospect did not meet with his approval.

"You'd think," I said bitterly, "that any normal person would be thrilled to bits to have their grandchildren staying. Look at Bill down the road always wheeling his grandson around and now he's bought him a junior motor car. Yellow," I added jealously, "and it actually goes." I knew that feeding three growing children would take all our resources and yellow motor cars were definitely out.

"He's only got the one," Tom replied gloomily, seeing his peace shattered, "and what about Malcolm? They'll frighten him off, you'll see, we'll lose him and bang goes your Christmas holiday," he added with relish as he departed for the garage to look under the bonnet of his car.

This pessimistic prophecy was not fulfilled for Malcolm was used to young people and organised them in a way I could not have done, we had more help not less. Liz pronounced him "a lovely man" but perhaps that was because he was always prepared to run her around and Liz was beginning to live her own life. The children had been to school here and had many friends, making friends was not a problem to them, as a travelling family they have always had a wide view of the world and friends were from many countries and were always coming and going.

I decided that the boys and I would visit Amanda in the Midlands, Liz stayed with friends, the sea was still very cold here and no-one seemed attracted to it. Peter, a year or two before, had looked at it in amazement and said, "It must be a very large lake." Now cold and forbidding with a late spring chilly wind we left it and drove northwards.

Amanda had decided to move, now where did I see the statement "never write about moving"? Everybody moves at some time or other, it is an experience everyone likes to share on the basis that their own event was much worse, it is often one of the great upheavals in an otherwise blameless life. Amanda found her present house too big, had sold it and found a small flat. What a situation for disaster. Fortunately we did not stay for the final turmoil, but we'd said we'd help, and as Amanda rushed off to work she said, "you could just turn out the shed."

It hadn't been disturbed for years. Adam found an old bicycle, Peter found a hammock, and among all the old tools and whatever-is-it rubbish I even found a box of dusty books, some of which I hadn't even read. It was a lovely day, there were two gnarled old apple trees bearing fruit and at just the right distance for the hammock. Peace reigned until Amanda returned and in disgust said, "It's the wrong shed."

Our stay was a short one, perhaps our help was not wholly appreciated but we successfully turned out another shed and went to a fancy dress lunch.

"Characters out of films," said Amanda. I had plenty of Asian looking clothes and announced that I was the wicked Mother-in-law from "Flowering Passion".

"I'm not dressing up," said Peter scornfully.

"No way," Adam backed him up.

"Two extras from Westside Story," I told our hostess who was too busy with the food to notice. When food was announced the 'two extras' were first there, it's a mistake to hang back when my family are around.

We'd given Tom a break and now thought we might return to him as the weather was warmer and outside activities would cheer him especially as they were all now more interested in looking under bonnets and changing wheels, gardening too especially with hose pipes, was an acceptable pastime.

There were other sports also, the sea did not look so unwelcoming and friends were urging visits and suggesting other enterprises especially with water.

Before long Simon and Jennie arrived and relieved me of responsibility. I was surprised at the end of their time when Liz said, "It's been a wonderful holiday."

"But you didn't do anything," I commented.

"I could if I'd wanted to." That is the difference between Pakistan and England, we can if we want to - a wonderful freedom.

"It won't be long before you're with us again," said Simon and we all looked at Malcolm now cheerfully realising the chief of his duties that of husband minding.

"Okay by me," said Tom, also cheerfully looking forward to doing his own thing. The family returned to work and school while I, once again, took up my various occupations and looked forward to rejoining them for Christmas.

Chapter 8

Return to Islamabad

I think I am getting too old to travel all night and into a different time. My hours are all mixed up and I am tired when I should be awake and, of course, awake when I should be sleeping.

"This will probably be my last trip," I said to Simon as he met me cheerfully at the airport.

"You say that every year," he replied, as shouldering my now usual motley collection of luggage, he jumped over a few barriers and hustled me into his waiting car. "You'll feel better after a good night's rest and then we're all going to a wedding."

"What, me as well?"

"You're asked, of course, but the boys don't want to go, they say it's too boring."

"Boring? A Pakistan wedding?" But I let it pass, no doubt I shall hear more when we reach the house.

I feel at home here and already find myself relaxing. The doubtful Joseph has departed having misguidedly started to sell off some of Simon's possessions and a couple have replaced him. Daniel and Martha are waiting with the family to greet me.

Jennie later said that she didn't send Martha to me but when there was a knock, my "Come in" brought Martha to my side. I was a little startled when pushing me on to the bed she started a massage routine, working up my legs and arms and even having a go at my head. She had very powerful arms and I found myself unable to resist and quite overpowered. Was she trained, I wondered, or merely practising mystical skills handed down through generations?

Amazingly I felt better and more able to cope with unpacking and finding all the articles requested by the young people which they had assured me were unattainable here. I doubted this after visiting the shops; I shall know better next time.

I now joined the family and the wedding discussion. The boys persisted in their determination to stay at home and mind 'grandma'. This idea appealed to me more than the wedding which Simon and Jennie were expected to attend. Liz had no intention of going, I decided to stay also as long as Jennie brought back full details.

"They know each other," Jennie said "so it won't be like the one we went to before."

"It was terrible," said Adam, "the bride wept buckets the whole time and it went on forever."

"It won't do for me," said Liz, "I like to see what I'm getting."

"You're too young to be thinking of such things," I told her firmly.

"Not here," she replied, "here, thirteen is a good age for marriage." She agreed with the boys that it was all boring, she retired to her room and shut the door. I felt I ought to go for the experience but I was sure Jennie would remember all the most interesting bits. The discussion ended with what Simon and Jennie would wear and what to take. They left early next morning, they would be away for two or three days.

Adam said, "Whatever you want to do we can do, we want to go shopping so Daniel has gone to get us a taxi. We can show you the best places."

I agreed to this arrangement, Christmas wasn't far away and I did appear to be the only one with any cash.

I wasn't surprised at their confidence and knowledge of these very Asian shops, they did know all the best places and how to bargain.

Elizabeth appeared to live her own life, only raising her head from her pillow to tell me 'not to' when I told her we were taking a taxi to Daman-e-koh, the look-out point in the Margalla hills.

"Why not?" I asked, being reluctant to obey my granddaughter. "Too dangerous," she replied and returned her head to the pillow, "Get a taxi," I said to Adam, "I could do with a bit of excitement and danger."

The twisty road was not more dangerous than usual, the taximan's determination to show us the monkeys and the occasional drifts of mist did, however, add to the excitement. The lookout was a washout owing to the mist but the boys had a drink at the café and agreed that a bit more shopping would be more fruitful. We had collected a following, all men and boys who wanted to talk English, oddly enough Adam and Peter seemed embarrassed, they had been so full of confidence that I was surprised at this, but they answered questions and smiled cheerfully at their interviewers. They are used to this attention, maybe Simon keeps the hordes at bay, I wasn't much use, no-one wants to question an elderly grandma.

Simon and Jennie returned with tales of this grand wedding, I listened enthralled. It had taken three days and they were both exhausted while I was now thoroughly rested.

"There were two tents," said Jennie, "one for the men and one for the women." I knew about these tents now, colourful and carpeted so I was able to imagine the scene. "The women had their hands painted with henna, the palms - that is - no-one knew why," she continued, "Simon was allowed in with me to the women's tent but they all covered their faces." How wise I thought, and a great advantage at my age.

"The men danced with transvestites," said Simon "as they can't dance with the women."

"There was a handing over ceremony, it was a love match so everyone was happy. The presents were all money, it was all counted and a list made of the amount," Jennie went on, "we didn't know this and wouldn't have given money anyway. Our gift was well received, our ignorance forgiven!" It seemed a bit mercenary to me, but I accept that customs differ.

I shouldn't have missed it but I was much happier watching the goings on from the balcony look-out and being shown around by the boys. We seldom met up with Elizabeth.

I was intrigued by the street cries that came from the road, I could watch from the balcony without being seen, the street cries came from sellers of various commodities, charcoal, oranges, themselves perhaps as I could see no goods on the makeshift carts. Perhaps a plumber or a mali, not a sweep or he would surely have some brushes. Back home I never see anyone carrying an obviously full teapot, this one was carried by a woman maybe for someone working further up the road or as refreshment for the chokidars who gathered in groups when the house owners were absent. We didn't have a chokidar as Daniel acted as man of all work except gardening or sweeping or giving Mama a massage!

Nobody in the road sang anything like a song I learned at school entitled "Who'll buy my sweet lavender", this was supposed to be a rendering of an old London street cry, maybe those old cries resembled these more raucous shouts.

One sound I couldn't ignore and shouted for the boys. They came running at the sound of music, it was a dancing bear.

"Yes," said Adam, "we've often seen it."

"Poor thing," said Peter, "perhaps we could buy it."

"Perhaps," I said "but could we take it home? Would the cats like it and what would it eat?"

"Cat food" suggested Peter.

"Or perhaps the cats," said Adam.

Such sights are frustrating, there is nothing one can do and no RSPCA.

Donkeys trotted by all day, these were being used to move rubble from a building site down the road, they looked well fed and fairly well treated. They carried baskets of stone and dust one way and returned well loaded with an overfed passenger who looked as if he could do with the walk.

Over the way a scruffy pup was tied to a gate, it barked endlessly and Adam and Peter tired of this and, feeling sorry for the pup, went over to ask if they could take it for a walk. The owner was away but the chokidar was only too pleased to be rid of his charge. It was a dirty little thing and the boys christened it 'Grub'.

"It is a bit grubby," I said "couldn't you wash it?" They were fondling and petting it.

"Great" said Adam delightedly and they rushed into their shower room, there was much laughter, the boys emerged soaked but the appearance of Grub was quite startling.

"Snowball," I suggested viewing this white pedigree-looking ball of fluff.

It caused a sensation when it was returned by the boys with as much drama as they could manage. Soon re-tied to its gate I wondered how long it would retain its perfect pristine appearance.

Also tied, this time by their legs, were chickens in our small local shopping centre, Muddy market is, perhaps a better description, small shops surrounding an unkempt uneven area which was perhaps meant to be green. I call these shops but they are more like large cupboards with iron gates that can be locked at night. These cubby-holes are crammed full of goods up to the roof. I supposed the owners knew where everything was for I could see no system. Among the grocers, green grocers, a fly-infested butcher and two video shops, was a small tailoring establishment where men were sitting outside cross-legged and engaged in their trade. The space in the cupboard behind being taken up with piles of materials and the chair of the boss who took the orders and the money. I was worried for the workers, where did they go when it rained? I didn't go to find out for the area outside was a quagmire and the inside was probably worse. The boys often visited this market and returned with different edible goodies.

"There's even ice cream," said Peter.

"Sometimes" added Simon.

"I don't like the live cooped-up chickens and the butcher" I said.

"We don't look at them, we're vegetarians," said Peter. But I did visit the tailor and very good and cheap he was.

One day watching from the balcony I witnessed the arrival of a snake-charmer. The little dog was barking wildly as the man settled himself nearby and brought out his pipe, the boys joined the admiring group now gathering round him and Adam sent Peter to me to ask for money.

"For the snake?" I asked.

"For the charmer," replied Peter.

How much for a snake charmer? We don't have many in our village. By one man I was seen and he called out to me.

"Madam, I am the mali but I am not coming today because I am having my teeth done." He opened his mouth wide, "See, this is the tooth I am having done."

I could not see from where I was so I shouted down encouragement, his teeth looked excellent to me. I did not think it would make much difference whether he came or not for with so little garden there was not a great deal to do except water and re-straighten my usual, to him, haphazard arrangement of pots.

I didn't think that Daniel and Martha's English was as good as Jennie had led me to believe. I was alone when Daniel came for money to buy polish. "Will you buy me some lemonade as well?" I asked, I knew the boys went to this market for drinks.

"Lemonade," he repeated, so I thought he understood.

"Are there any flowers there?" I now asked, thinking of a bowl of roses.

"Flower," he said, "Yes." Only Jennie explained the resulting batch of cakes to me.

"What did you ask for?"

"Flowers," I said.

"Flour means cakes," said Jennie. "And lemonade has to be called by its brand name."

Jokingly I said to Daniel, "You must come to England with me," knowing it couldn't happen and not expecting to be taken seriously. His English improved suddenly and he even thought I could take Martha on her own. The thought of endless massaging didn't tempt me.

"We have our own man," I said thinking of our Malcolm I'd never been able to say this before. Sadly he'd never offered massage.

Simon told Daniel that they would never get visas and I added that their place was here looking after my family. Honour was satisfied.

Perhaps it was my fault for I often failed to get my message over.

Simon came in at lunch time one day when he was feeling unwell. A real spread was put before us, Simon looked at this in disbelief, the table was loaded.

"What did you ask for?" he said accusingly.

"Bread and cheese," I answered. We looked at the table, no bread and no cheese. Simon gazed once more in horror, closed his eyes and went to sleep.

I agreed with Martha that Daniel was a good cook but she said this with such regularity even when he was cleaning the car that I did wonder if perhaps it was merely a phrase she had learned. I was puzzled when she repeated it as he was hanging out the washing, maybe I thought she was commending him and bringing him to our notice.

"Good wife," I said to Daniel pointing to Martha. Much laughter so I repeated "Good cook," to press the point. Even Jennie couldn't account for the batch of cakes again.

I had begun to worry as Martha became more and more my handmaiden, much as I'd always fancied this I felt I could get used to it too easily. My clothes washed, ironed and hung up and hardly allowed to lift a finger, I recognised that this was not really 'me'. I valued my freedom too much, I prefer to do up my own buttons as long as I am able to do so.

I found myself avoiding her as she lay in wait for me hoping to get in a little extra massage.

Daniel and Martha were Christians so at Christmas Simon gave them time off to visit relatives. Some friends of ours who were away too lent us their man to do the washing up. Simon cooked breakfast and we opened presents. I remember I had a warm Pakistani blanket which proved useful when we started our roving again.

If I thought this quiet family Christmas peace meant that there would be no cakes I was wrong. Later that day and most of the next they arrived along with the givers and their wives and families.

"Enough cakes for a picnic," said Simon, cheerfully viewing the leftovers from the inevitable party. "I've work to do in Muzaffarabad," he continued, "So we'll all go. We'll stay at the rest houses. If you like we can come back home by Rohtas Fort as Joy would like to see it."

There were protestations from the younger members of the family all of whom now had their friends and outside interests. The objections were waved aside and packing started. Jennie was determined on a break anyway and the good weather, - no snow, no rain - held.

It was a wonderful journey which improved as the day went on and we went upwards, the roads were fairly busy but this was of no great importance until we reached the narrower roads, then twisting and turning and with unprotected sides revealing immense drops. The appearance round a corner of a grossly overloaded bus was, to say the least, terrifying.

On the way up we stopped at a crowded hotel, this was obviously a favourite spot and the destination of most of the traffic. The car park was full, the restaurants were full - we had our own refreshments anyway - the hotel itself appeared to be full, the people here do like to congregate together. At the entrance was the tallest man I'd ever seen.

"It must be the one from the Guinness Book of Records," said Adam in awe. Adam is a great reader of this book and I am sure he was right.

"I hope I stop growing before I get there," said Peter, dolefully, as he looked up at this majestic figure. "I don't like the idea of endlessly opening doors."

We made for the loos which were also crowded and I was surprised in the 'Ladies' to find a man doling out the toilet paper. I found this odd in so segregated a society.

Peter had disappeared and was discovered with a large helping of candy floss. "I bought it at a stall," he said, waving his hand vaguely in an over-there direction.

We were in a hurry to leave this over-populated tourist attraction, after this there was very little traffic of the domestic type, it was just as well as the road became even more tortuous, at the same time the scenery became even more spectacular. There were still the heavy overloaded fancy painted lorries and the overcrowded fancy painted buses. On some of these the overcrowding spread to the top of the bus where young men held on precariously. I was horrified but Adam comforted me.

"Don't you see," he said, "They'll be the first to jump off if it goes over the edge, it's an advantage." Perhaps Adam has inherited his father's optimistic outlook.

During a drive it's normal for young people to talk, discuss, quarrel and generally fuss and so it was as we ascended. But suddenly I noticed a silence, we all looked fixedly ahead, there was no more racketing around and occasionally eyes were closed. This way I couldn't see over the edge to see the non-survivors for there must have been some for whom prayers were not enough.

There were trees on the slopes, "Enough," said Adam "to break the fall of a small car, or a biggish one, perhaps. Not a bus for that might uproot the trees."

I admitted the usefulness of the trees, yes one could perhaps cling to one, but I admired the trees also for their addition to the staggering beauty of the view as if framing the hills beyond the precipitous drops. These faraway snow-capped mountains were pink topped in the sun.

The trees, though, made the road dark and we were reaching the snow line but Simon still drove along it as if he had done it all his life.

"Actually," he said, when I thought a little praise was due, "I've done it seventy-two times and I'm heartily sick of it."

Peter said he felt sick anyway but no-one took any notice.

We arrived at Muzaffarabad at last, it was getting dark and it was cold. My room soon warmed up with a gas heater and I decided to stay in it rather than accept an invitation out that Simon had accepted on our behalf. At this point it was discovered that the car keys had somehow been shut in the car. I had decided wisely and an omelette was sent to my room wisely I thought as I saw the others waiting for transport in the cold. Later having found three quilts and had my hot water bottle filled with boiling water I drifted off to sleep. The man didn't understand the label that read 'Do not use boiling water' so the H.W.B. stayed hot all night.

I liked Muzaffarabad and later Jennie and I persuaded the cook, an extremely brigand looking man, to take us round the Fort. His appearance belied his character for in spite of a grim countenance he turned out to be a kind and helpful guide. He was also a good cook.

I loved the Fort which was probably once guarding the town, a wonderful flowing river divides here and small shops are pitched on the sides of the river banks. I wondered what held them there. The town seemed to be full of unsmiling men and I wondered about this too.

In these mountain towns there is a great temperature contrast, very cold nights but when the sun is up and in a sheltered spot it can be surprisingly hot. We found it so here and the lovely warm day with meals on the veranda became another cold night.

The sun was beginning to warm us up when we set off again next morning. The drive was even more spectacular, quite the most fantastic I'd ever been on, we could see the terracing now below us as we twisted and turned again on the road, there were more fir trees and more settled snow on the ground. In the distance beyond the dark hills the snow-capped mountains could again be seen.

Kashmir has a romantic sound and the countryside up to now fulfilled my expectations. I was surprised, therefore, at one point to see extensive road building with bulldozers, tractors, cement mixers and all the trappings of a vast enterprise, this alongside the endless sheer cliffs and the rushing river below.

After we had gone some way and the road was descending I thought longingly of refreshment.

"I could do with a drink," I said "preferably tea."

"I know a nice little open air café," said Simon, "we'll stop there."

Open Air Café! How refreshing and delightful it sounded, in my imagination I saw it, fresh air, colourful shrubs, greenery, overhanging trees. How different reality. It was open to a muddy stream that oozed its way over uneven stones. There was a rusty tin doorway leading inside and the traffic, for there always is some, squelched its way past. Goats and dogs rummaged in the rubbish. What might once have been a curtain dangled crookedly over the open door. The café hung on the usual slope where its debris was obviously thrown.

Everyone within stared at us as we groped our way through the grimy gloom. The metal wobbly tables were covered with grubby oilcloth. Simon pointed out the excellence of the place as he led us to an empty table and swept various bits on it to the floor.

"Do you come here often?" enquired Peter of his father as we gazed around. Simon ignored this and continued to extol its virtues.

"Bedrooms behind there," he said, pointing to some hanging rush matting which looked well past its sell-by date.

"You wanted tea," he said, "It's good here." Surprisingly it was! "Anyone want anything to eat?" he continued. We all refused. "If you're uncomfortable," he went on as I rocked on an uneven bench, "you can lean against the wall!"

I preferred not to but as I drank the very hot tea I gazed beyond the mucky slope to the great range of mountains, fresh, clean pure white and remote.

There were few tourists here but a small stall opposite enabled me to buy some biscuits - just in case.

I was clutching these at our next tea stop. I was a little wary this time when we were all clamouring for drinks again.

"Open air?" I asked when Simon said he knew just the place and it wasn't far. This one hung on the side of the road and the road was steep and slippery. Here we sat on some stone steps facing the road. Simon and I drank the mixed brew that is generally served as tea. It's a thick mixture with sugar and tinned milk not to be confused with the drink we know at home. The others preferred soft drinks.

"It's too sweet," said Liz, "but you have to have sugar in it to take away the taste of the milk."

It seemed a logical explanation. I handed round my biscuits and we watched the chickens, goats and a puppy scratching or playing in the dirt.

It was somewhere on the road and while passing through a town, the name of which I cannot remember, that Simon stopped the car, got out and embraced a passing man heartily.

"He's invited us to his house for tea," explained Simon. "A good man, a very good man."

Tea, I thought, obviously a good man if he can see that Mother is in need of tea. We all perked up, combed our hair and followed directions to the house.

We were left alone in a large room with chairs down either side, I suspect our host had to apprise the household of our arrival, we sat opposite each other and waited - and waited. Nuts appeared, fruit came, other dishes of spiced foods, men came and went bringing eggs, cakes, biscuits. I longed for tea. I could eat none of this. Cooked dishes began to appear, I was getting desperate although the others, more polite than I, were busy devouring these goodies.

The family arrived and with them tea at last!

The wife was presented and Simon with his knowledge of the normal household started to air his Urdu.

I intervened for luckily I had heard something of her. "Madam is an Oxford Graduate," I said to Simon. He apologised.

Her English was perfect.

I have made a note that the next rest house was spinach coloured and that we were the only guests. There were three floors descending in price as you ascended. Or - "Cheaper as you go up and considerably colder," explained Simon. There appeared to be no heating whatsoever. "They're not cold," he said bracingly as the children shivered, "they can jump about a bit."

He told us of a nice walk we could all go on "by a bubbling brook." No sparkling water here, it was a murky, slimy, struggling in its rubbish stream, but it was a walk and we did feel a few degrees warmer.

I had the only hot water bottle and I felt guilty as the sun went down but everyone wrapped themselves in blankets and anoraks, we looked more like a polar expedition than a family outing.

Before we left Islamabad everyone had said on hearing where we were going, "You're going up there, it's cold you know," or "It'll be cold up there." It was.

I could hear Liz's teeth chattering in the night, she had no cover. "Where's your duvet?" I asked her as I could see no sign of it.

"I gave it to a puppy outside," she replied, "it was cold and shivering."

Liz, Liz you silly darling, how could you, I said to myself as I went in search of other bed covers, we were the only guests so there had to be some. These I found in an unoccupied room and she fell asleep again. I never knew what happened to the puppy.

I woke early, hot tea was a necessity but I couldn't find anyone to make it. There were some unmoving blanketed lumps lying on chairs.

"Prod them and see," said Liz. I did and said "Tea." All sorts of noises started up, coughing, talking, rattling, even some music, maybe dancing warmed them up, eventually tea arrived.

All the family started to move, we planned to spend the day at the fort and still had some way to go. Breakfast was served in arctic conditions and we were wrapped up as before in everything we could lay our hands on. I did wonder if it would pay them to buy a few heaters.

The sun rose, the day warmed and we departed. Again the scenery was wonderful and the road hazardous but it did become warmer as we descended.

Chapter 9

Two Very Different Forts - Rohtas and Riwat

The family had visited Rohtas fort before and were going to show it to me. They were looking forward to this I think, for in one visit they had not seen all they wanted to see nor that they found all the gates to this amazing place. I had bought a small book about the fort by Ihsan Nadiem, an archaeological scholar who was obviously a lover of the place. I realised that I was not going to be able to see all of it in one short visit.

This isn't an easy place to get to and viewing the vast sandy plain that we had to cross I felt sympathy for an advancing or retreating army especially if the practice of pouring boiling oil on your enemies was in force then. The road ended suddenly and in front of us was what looked to me to be the beginning of a desert though I could see the fort in the distance.

"May I drive?" asked Adam, "Where to?" I asked myself but "Good place," agreed Simon, "not much traffic."

Not much! I couldn't see a single thing and would have welcomed a few other signs of life, perhaps other vehicles had been sunk in quicksand.

Simon moved over and Adam drove confidently and happily across the wilderness and then through a narrow river. There were tracks of vehicles either side of this stretch of water, we forded it here and arrived safely at the other side, eventually reaching one of the gates of the fort. There are twelve of these.

This approach is not only difficult but almost impossible after the rains as these flats are flooded. This flooding is not from the river - the river Kahan - but is a drainage channel filled with water flowing from the surrounding hills, it's known as a nulla. Now there was only this narrow river and other vehicles obviously came this way. One guide book suggests leaving the car when there is more water here for then it's safer to wade it. I never know my luck, I am glad to say I was spared this.

"It's fine now," said Simon, "I've only once had to turn back." Perhaps he didn't relish wading either.

Rohtas fort appears nowadays to be in the wilds and dominating a lonely spot but once it was on a main route and commanded a strategic position over the surrounding countryside. It seems strange looking at it now that such a place was of military significance but this must have been the case if the pass from the Northern Hills needed protection for it stands up on a rocky outcrop in the Kahan Gorge and must have been splendid in its time. What a wonderful site for a fort, it is one of the most surprising and impressive places that I have ever visited.

Sixteenth century Asian history is not one of my strong points, so I am relying on others for my information, but faced with such a building I do feel a natural interest and wonder who could have built it and why. The initiative came from Sher Shah Suri and it was an important place to prevent an attack from the Mughul Emperor which apparently never occurred. The history books tell of great deeds, no one tells of the daily chores. I should like to know, and probably never will, about the domestic side of this project. Who did the cooking and what did they eat. How many women were there and what did they do other than satisfy the needs of the men? The building must have employed many people and brought a certain amount of prosperity to the area but where did the money come from for all this work, for it must have cost a great deal? Someone said that the amount, or some of it, was written up on a door somewhere but I couldn't find it. Sher Shah must have been a very rich man for there would be the cost of his army as well, I suppose someone was always plundering and ransacking someone else. Whatever Sher Shah did or didn't do he must be remembered for this massive fortification.

I must recommend the guide books for descriptions of the fort, I only saw three or four of the gates and I did not climb on the ramparts.

The walls follow the contours of the rocks so the fortification has no particular shape, it's about three miles round and I'm not sure about the acreage within. The garrison would have lived here and there is still a small town.

"There are three hundred houses," Simon told me, "as well as schools and a post office."

I was surprised as I saw little of this as we wandered around. I wondered about bringing goods in after the rains, there must be some system. We did see a small mosque and Ihsan Nadiem writes of 'a flourishing bazaar'. He also says the town is unable to cater for the basic eating or drinking requirements - not to speak of other facilities of the visitors. This seems a pity and not impossible to remedy, there were so few tourists which in spite of the approach did seem extraordinary at so immensely a visitable place. Tourism does bring in money which helps with upkeep, but perhaps Pakistan doesn't wish to encourage tourists. This was not the first time I had felt sad at Pakistan's apparent indifference to its history. I had to admit I'd never heard of this fort before and it is a wonderful place.

I didn't notice any 'facilities' at all so I suppose the few visitors there found a convenient spot. If 'facilities' included a café it was minus stars, enterprise here could also help with upkeep. The difficult access is a deterrent but these days it is not an impossible task to cross a river and perhaps it is not only I who do not fancy wading. This is a place well worth preserving, there were some wonderful decorations that, sadly, may deteriorate if not looked after.

I think I should need a week at least to explore this whole area with its mighty wall and ramparts. The parts I did see were very fine, the gates varied from the most impressive to the back-door variety. I missed these less exciting entrances but the family showed me the baolis or water holes, a mosque and a building called a Haveli. I was fascinated by the baolis as these were dug down to the water level ensuring, as the rock was a lime rock, that there would always be water in time of siege. Modern reservoirs in fact.

We had brought our own picnic, we ate this under a great wall looking over the plains. It was sheltered and peaceful and we enjoyed sitting there in the warm sun as if we were waiting for an army that never came.

We had three punctures on the way home, I can't imagine how, one is usually too much for me. The resulting hold-up necessitated another overnight stop.

Somewhere along our route we had passed a great dam called the Mangla Dam reputed to be one of the largest earth filled dams in the world. It was impressive.

We stayed in the town of Jhelum, it was warm compared with our other stop-overs. I went shopping for some more biscuits and was served by a young man who not only looked me straight in the eyes but spoke with a Birmingham accent.

"Where do you come from?" I asked.

"Small 'eath," he replied.

"I know it well." I said.

I told Simon who thought that he'd been sent back here with new found Birmingham wealth. What better use for it!

John came in one Friday, guide book in hand.

"I've put up some sandwiches, I wondered if anyone would like to visit Riwat Fort?" Simon, Jennie and I were all free and this was a fort none of us had seen. But I said suspiciously, "What's in the sandwiches?"

"Peanut butter," replied John so I departed hastily to the kitchen to collect some rolls with cheese and tomato, a thermos flask and fruit. I am not into peanut butter.

John then read from the book, it said persuasively that it was 'a good place for a winter picnic being in good condition' and 'charming and peaceful'.

"Great," we said as we loaded ourselves and our supplies into his van.

"I've a tin of fish as well," John remarked viewing my supplies which looked like enough for a siege. Well - you never know.

The entrance to the fort didn't look encouraging, we climbed up a rough mound of dirt and rubbish, it was absolutely filthy, if anything it was worse inside as the noise was unbearable and the place was crowded.

We turned on John, "The book did say there was a mosque inside, and it is Friday ... " he muttered. None of us had realised that it was a working mosque but this hardly accounted for the unattractive surrounds. There was certainly no room for a picnic, there wasn't a clean spot to spread our rug and added to our discomfort there were a crowd of small children following us giggling and pushing.

"No thank you," we said but Simon, walking about in disgust added, "I know a nice little stupa."

It's curious how Simon seems to know exactly where he is and knows just the 'right little place'. How could he know 'a nice little Stupa' in the middle of nowhere? He directed John to this deserted quiet stupa, not a soul there, perhaps they were all in the mosque. The stupa was indeed all alone, we walked around and up it and then spread our rug by the track, only a camel went by.

Looking in the guide book I was intrigued to see that we were near the Soan Valley or Gorge, a place renowned for its fossils of early man and many animals. Enquiries produced blank stares, no-one seemed to know anything about it. I decided to ask George on my return as he'll probably know all about early settlements here. Pity I had to wait though, as I was there. But where? It looked a long scrambling journey of discovery. John said he thought he knew somebody who once said he'd heard of it ... George, where are you?

My time was running out again but this time I was not the only one leaving. Simon's contract had finished and all was confusion in the house and in our minds. He had managed to sell the furniture and now these assets were beginning to look somewhat shop-soiled. 'No feet on the sofa' became a rule, polishing, mending, cleaning and recovering made us all feel exceedingly temporary.

New consultancies were offered to Simon and I answered the phone to a definite and anxious offer of an 'excellent opportunity in Nigeria'.

"Never again," was Simon's verdict.

The time I was there I'd enjoyed Nigeria, but I got his point.

Another was offered in Islamabad again but I knew the family wished to move on. Simon had begun to think of wider interests and different possibilities. He wanted to move forward and use gained knowledge in a progressive way.

"If it's Nigeria," he repeated, "tell them No, there's no need to refer it to me." I knew he'd applied for one in India.

"Don't suppose I'll get it," he said, "too many good people, but it's the one I want."

No Mother could agree that others might be better than her son.

He was determined that I should 'do' one or two more trips before I left.

"Tell me when you want to go," he said as we tripped over carpets, the polisher and the Urdu teacher who, fearful of losing his pupil seemed to be taking up permanent residency as he sat in the warmth and watched television. His main use at this time was translating to the various workmen who came and went and particularly to Daniel and Martha who were in great distress as they viewed indications of departure. They made many requests through his interpretation to be my servants in England, even though Simon and Jennie had given them to understand that they would not be deserted but another post would be found for them. My ideas of a handmaiden had long since faded.

I wanted to see Taxila again and we left, though only for a day, the thorough confusion of my packing and imminent departure, of Liz's trying to tidy her room which was reminiscent of a jumble sale and the boys' oblivion of the various activities as they migrated to the television, ignoring the Urdu teacher and his obvious determination to bring in his whole family.

We went then to the peace of this ancient civilisation which, in its day, was probably just as full of bustling activity as the scene we had left behind us. I love these archaeological sites and Taxila had very much caught my fancy. Visiting sites such as these isn't everyone's cup of tea but Pakistan is full of interesting archaeological wonders. I am no expert but I think it would be strange not to visit at least one,

Taxila is one, Moenjodaro is another well worth a visit and Taxila is one of the best preserved.

We drove through abundantly laden orange groves and I admired the roadside stalls banked up with the colourful fruit.

"On the way back ..." said Jennie, she didn't need to finish, we all had ideas of loading up and guzzling to our hearts content.

We went first to Sirsukh, this was a town built instead of Sirkup which had been ruined by an earthquake and been smitten by plague. We wandered around here for a while and then went up the valley to Mohra Moradu, this place really attracted me, there was a guide here who requested money, gave out tickets and was prepared to show us some of the protected and well preserved statues and specimens, one a beautifully kept small stupa. I am in favour of money collections as a means of helping in the upkeep of these places. This guide was quiet and unobtrusive, the place was peaceful, there was no one else there and we could see for ourselves the beautiful walls and the general layout, I was intrigued by the canal under the rocks although the guide was doubtful about its use.

We returned home by the orange sellers, as we stopped to buy a small car drew up and Simon welcomed the inhabitants as friends, they had to be introduced and one by one climbed out of the car. There were ten of them and a baby.

I was sorry to be leaving Islamabad, the streets are wide, the traffic bearable and the driving terrible, "But they're always so nice about it," said Simon after another near miss with resulting smiles all round. I was now used to the shopping areas and was able to walk around our own district without getting lost. The houses are built on a grand scale, some grander than others but all different so that I could say to myself 'left at the one with pillars, right at the red roof'. Others had flat roofs or large verandas, some had pink tiles, some were spinach coloured, some had barking dogs and most had iron gates. Knocking one down and building another mystified me but this practice seemed to be fairly common, perhaps they were not well built. I think someone told me that the land was taxed rather than the house which would account for the cramming in of a large house on a small plot.

All over the Indian subcontinent the love of design may be seen, it is a heritage not neglected but still carried on. An art teacher at the school where my grandchildren went was teaching these intricate, geometrical designs very different from the large freestyle ideas of art teaching back home.

Beautiful displays of fruit and vegetables may also be seen in the markets, even here the love of design is obvious and arrangements seem to show great artistic taste.

We had an earth tremor one morning. I wondered what was shaking my bed but going out saw that others were equally worried. It wasn't serious but enough to acquire an understanding of what a real quake could be like.

Martha was more worried about my departure than about earthquakes, if I forgot to lock my door she would be there at my feet with a "no problem my Mother," or massaging my legs if I was so unwise as to put them in an accessible place. Adam entered one day and seeing my predicament entreated me in anxious tones, "Could you come please, I need help with my homework?"

"Thank you," I said when outside and to myself "Blessed boy, here is one who will go far."

Best of all about Islamabad was its position with the Margalla hills rising up to the edge of the town.

"We'll do a walk there on the Friday before you go," promised Simon.

"What's this Joy walk I keep hearing about?" I asked, "John spoke of going up happiness and down joy."

"It's the walk you did last year of course," replied Simon, "don't you remember?"

A walk in the Margallas named after me, fame at last!

This time we went further and I was able to see the extent of this range with the sweep of the hills stretching away into the distance, its small farms and trees adding to the interest of what had so far to me been only a line of hills behind the town.

There were last minute shopping sprees and a fine party given by John for me with presentation roses and a beautiful pen. I know it was very unlikely that I should visit Islamabad again.

The family would follow me home soon until such time as Simon's new locality was known.

I said my 'goodbyes' and returned home once more.

Chapter 10

A Sad Return

I do not intend to dwell on sadness. There is too much terrible tragedy all around us that my own personal grief seems insignificant beside it.

Tom seemed fine when I returned, his phone calls and letters were cheerful and all pointed to a quiet uncomplaining winter, he hadn't been out as he now had no need to do so, Malcolm had shopped as well as other household duties while bearing in mind that Tom was a man who liked his personal space.

I'd had a wonderful break, but it was lovely to be home. Tom had been looking forward to my return, the Spring and getting out in his car again. The time with him was all too short, he deteriorated rapidly and died quietly in hospital shortly after my return, both Simon and Amanda arrived, I was glad we were able to be with him.

Tom was a peaceful person, he didn't like travel and disruptions to the smoothness of his life - such as Christmas.

So long as he didn't have to come he was quite happy for me to travel and spend Christmas elsewhere. He was quiet reliable, studious and a lover of music and mathematics. He was faithful, honest and predictable, not such very bad characteristics in a husband. We had long ago agreed to differ on some things and not to make a song and dance about it.

This very short chapter also ends a chapter of my life.

I am an admirer of Jane Austen and decided not to be like Mrs Dashwood and Marianne in 'Sense and Sensibility' who "gave themselves up wholly to their sorrow" and "encouraged each other in the violence of their affliction." I think this would be rather boring to other people and I tried from the beginning to reflect on all the good things that had gone before in our marriage, some of the wonderful times we had had as well as the not so good bits, times apart and, viewing our time together as a whole, I tried to think of it in terms of the continuation of my own life. I was not "resolved against even admitting consolation in future." I did not renew the "agony of grief" ... "again and again"!

Grief and remembrance is always there, one learns to live with it.

I was lucky in having my family.

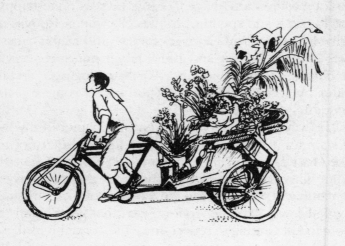

Chapter 11

New Delhi

"You'll love New Delhi," said a girl on the phone, a student in England who was returning home. "It's Diwali soon too, such fun." I was greatly cheered at this, I felt I could do with some fun and, as the plane came in to land and I saw the ground of India come up to meet us, I felt new hope for, very soon, I should be with my family again.

I had let our cottage and restlessly moved from one place to another, a mistake I now realised.

The family were home briefly in the summer before they moved to New Delhi where Simon now had a new contract. George arrived to help me achieve some sort of order in our cottage before letting it to holidaying tenants. We had collected so much junk, at least I had. Tom was not 'into' junk. George brought all his friends to 'help' as well so it could hardly be called a dull time. George's friends are rather large and have appetites to match their size, they were enjoying more fresh air than they were used to. The Aga was in constant use and I was too busy to mourn. It's a good time to learn one's real friends, those endlessly supportive, helping or just being there.

Summer holidays for the family ended, as they left Simon said, "It won't be long before you're with us again, you can stay as long as you like, I hope," he added, "we haven't found a house yet."

Frequent phone calls advised me of their progress in this direction and I tried to be as encouraging as I could as I looked forward to this visit, especially as the autumn mists descended on us and the nights grew longer.

Now, as the plane descended, I felt new hope, I had left the stressful time behind me, I should be meeting new people, strangers at first with whom I should make friends and be sharing experiences. I should be visiting new places, walking in distant hills (hopefully) or simply shopping in the astonishing, colourful and varied markets. I brighten at the prospect for I had loved India on my one brief visit. Now here it was again, I parted from my new 'Diwali loving' friend and there were Simon and Jennie to meet me.

But my first experience in Delhi was not one I had anticipated. I had arrived very tired and had gone to bed almost immediately, I slept late and heard the family depart. I surfaced and decided on a shower, on trying to return to the bedroom the handle of the door came off in my hand, the door was immovable. How to get out now became a problem. I had no idea of the layout of the house and the only very narrow window seemed totally inadequate. I banged and banged on the unresisting door to no avail. I shouted and shouted with the same non-result, I returned to the window, it was too narrow for me to squeeze through, but it opened and I had a view of the guard, I called and waved a hand and managed to sound urgently frantic, necessary in case he was not an English speaker. He probably had no idea of my problem but he fetched the couple who look after the family. This was my first meeting with Hari and Munju so their first impression of poor 'Mother' was a distressed figure draped in towels. They made shocked noises at my predicament but Hari was practical and rushed to phone a suitable workman. Tea was hastily brought to me and soon after I reappeared as respectable as a mother should be, breakfast was served while the hastily summoned locksmith tut-tutted over the bad workmanship of the door fitments. I wondered how long it would have taken back home to achieve such immediate results.

I had time now to relax and look around me. I tried to remember the names of this excellent bowing couple, yes - here it was in a letter. Simon had written before I left. Hari was the bearer and Munju the cook. Simon had written that they were hill people from the Nepalese borders, born on the Indian side so Indian. I had already met the driver - Thompson.

"Why Thompson?" I asked.

"He's a Christian," I was told.

Hari and Munju were Hindus and later introduced us to the fun time of Diwali, the festival of light.

"Like your Christmas," they said. It seemed, when Diwali came, much noisier than Christmas as firecrackers, easily available and much in evidence, didn't seem to me to have much to do with light.

My first impressions of the house and garden were mixed. I thought I had better explore and get my bearings, the house was bigger than I had expected. Carpets and furniture were still arriving, some curtains were up, it was all pleasantly expectant.

"I still haven't got a wardrobe," complained Peter, "How can I be tidy without a wardrobe?" I felt I was lucky to have a bed, it looked comfortable, I also had a large built in cupboard as well as reliable door handles! The rooms were big and airy with fans and air conditioning, necessary in the heat of summer, the weather now in October was pleasantly warm. It was a wide house too, with a central staircase and a most inviting banister from roof to basement. I never saw the boys walk down the stairs, one leg over and down, down round the perilous bends, the faster the better. I didn't try it myself, my bedroom being on the ground floor I hadn't a great need, I soon discovered the roof so I suppose this method of descent could have come in useful had I made an effort and no-one was looking.

Simon, in describing the house, had said that its position was a very noisy one, the noise came from the nearby main road and from planes as it lay in a flight path. The choice had been between this one, big but noisy, and a smaller, inconvenient moderately quiet one. They had chosen the bigger one and, when carpeted, curtained and the outside wall built up to twelve feet it wasn't so bad. Simon had also said, "Bring earplugs" and I had brought a good supply of these to find that the family wanted them for swimming, the noise of the house having been forgotten by the time I arrived. For a day or two I thought I should never get used to it but, like the sound of the waves crashing on the beach at home, which is now only background noise, this noise too soon went unnoticed. The nights were comparatively quiet as no heavy lorries were allowed on the roads and there was little horn tooting. It was on the roof that I noticed the noise most. In other houses I had made roof gardens, here not only was it so noisy it was, I thought, uninteresting. I was much mistaken, below me were still all the activities of a small Indian community and I soon learned to ignore the noise while watching the life below. At the corner was a little stall, attached to it was a wooden desk like structure that was removed every night. The stall consisted of a table with bowls and mugs, daily a fire was built and cooking took place, obviously the local cafe, what was cooked I never discovered but it was always busy. There were various carts piled high with peanuts or bananas, these were made of old bicycle wheels, crude but adequate, each seller had a different street cry. There were holes being dug and once some drainage work dug deeper than usual as smelly water overflowed. Holes were sometimes filled in, sometimes not and so potholes abounded. Wires hung everywhere and dangerous bits of pipe blocked the road. Strangely everything in the house seemed to work. There are wonderful parts of Delhi where tourists go with wide roads, fine views, green lawns and everything as it should be but there are many parts not like that where even the pavements are dangerous. The walkers here consisting of brightly dressed women, school children and strolling men, all of these seemed to prefer walking in the middle of the road.

There were others in the workforce at the house as well as Hari and Munju. The driver, Thompson, didn't clean the car, this was done by a youth in the early morning, the same youth occasionally helped the Mali who appeared at odd times with or without assistants. A sweeper came every day to sweep around the house, raise the dust and chat to Munju. Given a chance she swept around my feet if I sat on the balcony, it was all very lively. The Chokidars worked a shift system so that there was always someone at the gate.

There was to be an office party and I decided to visit the flower stall up the road, flowers are easy to buy here and this stall had looked tempting. It was a most successful jaunt; men, hidden away behind various boxes and structures, suddenly appeared, flowers were waved before my eyes, then arranged, cut to size and finally wrapped, a rickshaw was called as I was loaded with blooms and I was escorted to it after a presentation of a single red rose. My appearance back at the house laden with flowers startled Hari and Munju who hurriedly brought all the containers they could find.

I spent the rest of the day arranging them for the party in the evening. This was in the garden and we had outside caterers. As there was no washing up and, as everyone kept taking me aside to sing the praises of my son, it was a wonderful party.

I've said that Diwali, the festival of light, isn't quite like our Christmas, there was present giving and shrines but I didn't like the fire crackers. We were invited by Hari and Munju to see their decorations. Hari changed suddenly from the serious worker to an Indian dancer, and, as he showed us a dance, his eyes lit up and he gracefully swayed to the rhythm of the music. I tried not to think how Malcolm Fish would look if taught this beautiful exotic dancing. Perhaps not, perhaps Morris dancing would be more suitable.

Chapter 12

The Apple Valley

"Do you want to come into the hills with me?" asked Simon shortly after my arrival.

He didn't need to ask, I was already mentally packing and, before long, doing it with enthusiasm and putting in plenty of warm jumpers. I had been into the hills before.

Although I was now accustomed to the noise of Delhi, I found that the polluted air was not conducive to easy breathing, the thought of some clean air was very attractive.

It was some years since I had flown among the mountains and I had forgotten how beautiful it was, it all seemed so close, too, in the small plane whose wings almost seemed to touch the mountain sides. Everywhere were dotted the little homesteads and farms with terraced fields in amazingly high places. Beyond were glimpses of the white topped mountains shining in the sun in contrast to the dark ridges of the near hills which rose through the mist. Meandering paths could be seen connecting the dwellings and fields. It was a beautiful day and I was glad to be travelling again. We progressed up the valley where every available piece of land seemed to be cultivated. It was a small airport and there appeared to be a reception committee, obviously someone was expected. I looked around me at the disembarking passengers, who among them ...? A shock wave passed through me as I saw my son striding purposely forward and the truth dawned - it was for us and I wondered what they thought of the man who brought his Mother along. Everyone was so kind, I was ushered into the only waiting room and the welcoming noises and handshakes went on around me. Wait long enough, those of you with troublesome teenage sons!

We were driven uphill through the town to our hotel, this was a pleasant surprise as it might have been a glitzy showpiece instead of the pleasant, tasteful, modest building with rooms in the grounds which were reminiscent of Swiss chalets. The grounds sloped down to a river and I promised myself an exploratory walk when I had settled in. "Do whatever you want," said Simon as he dashed off to a meeting, "I'll be back this evening."

For a while I sat out on my balcony and breathed deeply. Just to be able to breathe this mountain air was a bonus after Delhi, and I had several days to explore and enjoy the valley - this lovely apple growing valley. And apples there were, and a few goats and an angora rabbit or two, it looked like a cottage industry with wool and looms in the cottages as well as apples and I found when I visited the shops that the Kulu shawls were beautiful. I couldn't resist these and the hats that the men were wearing - round with an attractive coloured border. I bought apple juice as well and found it superb. I was told that olive trees grew here but I didn't see any.

I had expected it to be cold and packed plenty of suitable warm clothes. No-one had warned me that at mid-day it could be hot, and it was. The sun came out and it was sunbathing weather. The beauty of the place was enhanced by the brightness and the almost blue shadows. There were firs on the far hills and this rushing river. I watched it cascading between the rocks, it seemed fairly fierce to me but was obviously relatively calm for there was evidence of some previous destructive descents, signs of torrents which had broken paths and moved great concrete blocks. There was a much destroyed platform for white water rafting and it looked like an excellent place for this sport. It also looked as if the river had greater sport of its own in its headlong dash down the river bed ruining everything in its downward path and causing great stones and blocks to fly. There wasn't much left of the rafting construction and much would have to be done before this sport could start again.

Later Simon visited this river rafting site with me. "I'll bring the family next time," he said looking at the flowing water, "They'll love it."

"Wait until it's patched up," I suggested and thought that Jennie might not be so enthusiastic as she watched her family disappear round the bend.

I wondered when all this damage had occurred but on wandering around the hotel compound I thought it had been fairly recent for some of the chalets had been flooded and damply ruined carpets had been dragged into the sun. I returned to the river and walked up the side of the river bed and tried to imagine the frightening sight of all this water gushing and racing downhill towards the town. Perhaps they are lucky as there seemed no water shortage.

In my room was an amazing contraption in a chimney nook. I had never seen anything like this magnificent fire holder. It was round and banded, it looked big enough to heat a banqueting hall, it was a monstrosity and I viewed it with misgiving. Evening brought a definite chill to the air, it also brought a young man to my door, he stood there carrying the materials for fire lighting, so the contraption was used. I looked at the large burn holes in the carpet and hastily reassured the youth that I was going out and would not be needing a furnace. He looked sad, I thought so perhaps he looked forward to the time when the place burned down. Later on in the year I expect it was very much colder here but, in October, I decided I would manage with my hot water bottle. However there was an electric heater which I thought looked marginally safer until I examined it closely and saw many bits of loose wire and joins of doubtful safety. I suggested to the young man that he brought me another which I would use for the short time I was occupying my room, the speed with which he did this suggested that it was a straight swap with the next door room. Oh well - hopefully the occupier was an electrician.

It was an evening party with all Simon's contacts turning up and no-one else in the hotel was served. I felt a million, also a bit guilty.

"We'll have our own party on Friday," said Simon. Whose party was this I wondered? It seemed to involve a lot of people, how different would 'our own' be.

In my wanderings about the valley I met a strange man, wildly bearded, bedraggled and with wonderful eyes. I wrote in my diary that he had a devil stick and a drum, he was beating the drum when I met him and this stick was only a branch hung with odd bits and pieces. There was a large flat stone by the side of the road. "Sit" he said, and we sat. This word may have been the only English he knew but I shall never know for we sat peacefully in silence. I compared sticks, mine had been a present from Amanda who had insisted I had one 'just in case'. The devil stick had been cut from a tree, mine was made of the latest unbreakable material, had a special spiked end, an excellent handle and adjustable to size joints. Alas it had no seat which was why I was sitting on a wayside stone with a mystery man. Was he a leper? Was that the drum's use, as a warning? Was he just a beggar though he didn't seem to be begging? Where had he come from, where did he live? Or to him was I the mystery? I hoped those beautiful eyes weren't blank and that there was no mind behind them. I'd sat long enough, I felt in my pockets, I had a few rupees. With what I hoped was great dignity I rose, presented my gift, touched him on the forehead and blessed him. Well, why not that way round? He too, received with dignity, bowed and went on his way. I returned to the hotel. I had tea and some wonderful apple juice in a dim coffee bar and waited for Simon's return. I didn't tell him of my encounter, he would have said "You shouldn't talk to strange men."

Many of the guests at our party were forestry experts and I'd hoped to find out about species and soils but I think Mothers are not expected to want to know such things and although I was treated with deference I was not able to satisfy my curiosity, my questions as to types of tree in relation to altitude were not answered. There were however unexpected (to me) speeches and I was presented with a beautiful Kulu shawl, fortunately words did not desert me for a thankyou speech. A young English woman consultant was also presented with a shawl, she was dressed in the usual drab clothes and jeans, as she threw the lovely salmon pink shawl over her shoulders she looked like a butterfly emerging from a chrysalis. Simon was given a hat.

We left next day, up to then there had been very few other guests at the hotel, now it was filling up and noisy families were moving in. I wish we could have stayed longer for a friend I met at our party told me about the Dussehra festival held here every year. I was always being told about festivals, those I'd met so far seemed very noisy for the Indians seem to have a love of fire crackers, a love I don't share.

"It's not like that," this friend, Rupa, said, "You would so enjoy it, there were only a hundred Gods 'brought' here last year but there used to be 365." It seemed a lot of Gods to me.

"They come from the plains in procession," Rupa continued, "thousands come to see it, it's very colourful, it lasts for a week."

"Where do all these Gods and processions go?" I asked as I hadn't seen that much space. I'd missed it, of course.

"I'll show you next time you come," Rupa said, "the Dhalpur Maidan is a large area, this is the valley of the Gods you know." Yes, I should have known.

I was cheered at the idea of there being a next time. I read somewhere that these festivities are the only things worth visiting in this valley. I decided many years ago not to accept other people's ideas for my views of this valley were entirely different. I saw one or two tempting little places where I wouldn't have minded setting up my own cottage industry and sit spinning in the doorway. I'm not sure about the winter though.

We flew home among the mountains again, and I wondered once more about the remote homesteads and who lived in such lonely and isolated spots.

I hoped that there would be other mountain trips and I didn't have long to wait.

Chapter 13

Shimla

"We're all going to Shimla," announced Simon expecting the usual opposition. There was none, no-one said "But Dad..." All wanted to go to Shimla especially as they had heard discussion on the amazing little hill train. It was a public holiday so all were free. Liz said she thought some of her friends were likely to be up there which explained her enthusiasm.

"It's the only train I know where you can hang out of the doors," said Simon longingly, "you can't do that in England, it's something I've always wanted to do." The boys agreed with their father that hanging out of trains was also one of their lifelong ambitions, it sounded dangerous and I pretended not to be interested. I certainly wanted to go on that train as I'd read a good deal about it. Flying suddenly seemed very dull compared with that splendid little narrow gauge railway.

We caught the wide gauge train from Delhi to Kalka, the mountain train starts its remarkable journey here. Delhi railway station needs a chapter on its own but for now I shall only say that I clung to Simon who seemed to know where he was going, I think he was following a red shirted porter, we all arrived safely on the right platform and found our named seats. Booking is essential.

At Kalka we boarded our train for the hill journey up to Shimla.

Shimla, known in the days of the British as Simla, became the seat of Government officially in 1847. Before then, I imagine, as many people as possible drifted up to the cooler hills when hot Delhi and life on the plains became unbearable. The train was planned as the journey before then was hazardous, the carrying up of mountains of luggage being a momentous undertaking. The railway was opened in 1903, the distance up the slope meant many tunnels and bridges as the track zig-zags upwards.

It's a lovely little train, we boarded it at Kalka and sat back to enjoy the journey. 'Sat back' - no way - there was all this hanging out of doors to be gone through, it was more exciting than I had expected because other parts of the train could be seen as we curved around the track and we could wave to each other from another doorway, it was hardly an express, just a pleasant chug. There was no feeling of haste, food was served as well, though I have forgotten what it consisted of, probably omelettes. It was a great journey taking about six hours. It should have been less but we were held up for a time for a train coming in the opposite direction.

Adam had all the statistics.

"There are 102 tunnels and 869 bridges," he said. I didn't argue and my counting was spasmodic. Was our counting at fault for we found one to be missing, No. 46 wasn't there and the tunnels were marked to 103. What happened to 46 I wonder?

What an engineering feat this was.

Shimla was the most important of the hill stations as it was the summer capital. "Left over from the British" someone described it. Yes, there are some Britishy bits about it, it's an attractive town, which lies in a crescent around the mountain sides.

It was dark however when we arrived, found a Taxi and wound our way around the usual bends to our hotel.

I was offered a room on the ground floor or one on the second floor, I chose the latter, thinking that warm air rises. I needn't have bothered, it was arctic and perhaps the ground floor might have had a flow of warmth from the kitchen. The room had a heater and I had a hot water bottle, the rooms also had television and after supper we all braved the long Siberian corridors and went to bed.

Everything warms up with the sun and next morning it looked like a promising day, the sun was shining in through my window and enhancing the old fashioned look of the heavy furniture and making patterns on the bathroom floor so that I even considered washing. Breakfast was liberal and soon warmed us up before we set out to explore the town. I can't compare the town with how it used to be for I was never there, it is now a popular resort in summer and a completely Indian town. We walked across the Mall and to Scandal point, here there were pony rides and a wonderful view, I wonder why it reminded me of Weymouth front, just a feeling of promenading I suppose.

"Someone was abducted from here," Jennie told me, "Kipling wrote about it." I had to be content with that, it was now crowded with people and didn't look at all scandally.

"There is a Britishy feeling about the town," I said to Simon.

"And why not," he said, "they practically invented the place." The building of the railway certainly put it on the map. We lost Liz sometime during the day, she found friends and decided to stay with them, this way she missed Simon's great walk the next day.

The plan for this walk included me but I was not to walk across the hills.

"Too rough, too steep, too cold," said Simon. "We'll have a taxi to start and you can continue on in it," he pointed to the map, "it'll drop us here and we'll meet up on the road - here, then it drops us - here, drives you to - here and comes back for us - here. We all eat there and all come home in the Taxi." Um-err! Where exactly?

It sounded fine, but I didn't have the map and most of the day I had no idea where I was. Not that it really mattered in the amazing scenery as we twisted and turned among the hills, though I did think, once or twice, that I might be safer walking. There was no hurry but the driver was determined to show me his skills, after a time I opened my eyes as I was determined not to miss the excitement of it, the wonders of the hills and the distant snows.

The mountain roads here are just as hazardous as those in Pakistan and the views are just as beautiful, rushing streams, a mixture of fine firs, some of them deodars, and the far off hills bleak and daunting. The houses too perched on mountain sides, appear to have only tracks. Adam had told me that the highest cricket pitch in the world is in India, he appears to have an endless knowledge of curious facts but had no idea what happened if someone hit a boundary if the pitch is on the side of a hill for, as in Pakistan, there is always a game going on in unlikely places.

We stopped by a small waterfall and a rag covered shack on poles, was this another open air café I wondered? I stayed in the taxi and ate my snack while the driver joined the group outside this ramshackle place. The waterfall was probably the reason for the habitation for pots and old oil drums were filled from it and a small bottom was sluiced down under it. The water looked clean but cold, the small child shivered, the pool beneath the fall did not look inviting.

I waited patiently until I heard shouts and I spotted the family descending the mountain, the driver came running and we had completed stage one.

Stage two consisted of a short taxi ride along the road until the others found the mountain trail again and I taxied on to the hotel where we should meet, eat and complete the day with the drive home.

I was abandoned at this hotel so I wandered in the gardens, had coffee and watched the antics of the monkeys.

We had seen monkeys at Shimla. "Don't encourage them," said Simon.

I saw what he meant here in the hotel gardens where two young men appeared to be employed solely to throw stones at them so that they didn't worry the guests. The guests, however, encourage them, it's a novelty to have monkeys at your table and, only after your meal has been snatched from you do you call for assistance, especially when it becomes obvious that others advancing to the feast are going to be more than a nuisance, possibly a menace. Later I watched while all these monkeys and their friends and neighbours were fed food from the hotel that was thrown down the side of a hill, there was a great clamouring and hullabaloo as the throng collected for its meal.

The sun was beginning to set when the taxi departed to fetch the walkers on the last stage but one. The final stage was the ride home. It was beginning to get cold and I was beginning to worry when they arrived for a hot meal and drinks. They were cold having left jumpers with me and I was cold as usual at night and at this height in the hills.

When I was sitting waiting for the walkers I remembered meeting a man in the Margalla Hills who said, "I take off my hat to you." Nobody, I thought, should be taking a hat off to me now, I should be out there walking with them. Now, on our return journey we saw horses by the dozen saddled and with their attendants, it was getting dark and they, too, were returning home.

"Next time," I told Simon, "that's what I'll do, I'll hire a horse or pony and ride with you." The guide book said nothing about pony trekking.

"This isn't the India of old," replied Simon, "When your syce awaited you, how do you get your mount to the starting point?"

"I'll have to think it out," I said, not wishing to abandon my project.

"These days," confirmed Simon, "it's more likely that your driver has lost the car keys." I agree, this is modern India but all the way home we meet these groups of hopeful horses and I continue to dream of a mountain ride.

As we drove home it became colder still and as we climbed higher there was snow on the roads, it seemed to be a different route from the one I'd been on earlier in the day and I was shivering with cold when Peter shouted, "There's a Yak here!"

We stopped and the others rushed into the gloomy woods, I was huddled further into my coat when Simon returned.

"You're not going to miss this," he said, "You're going to see it even if I have to carry you."

Agreeing that I might never have an opportunity again of seeing a Yak, I reluctantly followed him. I had not expected it to be so magnificent a beast, it was enormous, black and beautiful, I wouldn't have missed it for worlds there in these woods in the cold, cold hills, huge, placid, quietly eating.

I was heaved back up the slopes, half dragged, half pulled back into the taxi and we returned to Shimla.

We had the same taxi driver when we left Shimla to go home to Delhi but we decided not to go by the little train, instead we drove down to Chandigarh on the main line to Delhi.

The taxi arrived and we waited patiently in it while Simon shouted for Liz to hurry up, Liz is always the last to arrive and as she had not been on the walk the driver had not seen her before and thought, impatiently, that the party was complete. When the apparition arrived, red hair floating behind, still clutching a toothbrush and loudly protesting he was dumbfounded, his expression conveying his thought 'is she part of this group?' For a moment he seemed paralysed at the sight and I hoped he would keep his eyes on the road. On the whole he was a good driver and it was a long difficult drive and necessitated swinging the wheel left and right while negotiating the endless bends, if he had a tendency to open his car door and shout to his friends or glance too frequently backwards to see if the vision was still with us who can blame him, it must have added variety to a route he probably knew well. We hoped so when we saw wheels of overturned vehicles down the steep sides of the road. There were monkeys sitting on the walls all the way down especially where a hotel perched on the hillside, they looked thriving and there were many babies.

We arrived in good time in Chandigarh, at first sight and with very few travellers the station looked a bit like Bournemouth Central but the idea faded as the people began to arrive and collect on the platform, the crowds were colourful, jostling and pushing, I began to notice other events unlikely in Bournemouth, on the track a cow wandered followed by a herd of goats, a bitch and two pups looked likely to fall under the next train, passengers from which when it arrived just jumped off it onto the track and walked away in various directions. A man came and stared at Liz for so long I began to think of Amanda in Egypt and I wondered if camel bartering extended to India and what I might accept if he made an offer. Sadly he went away, perhaps he realised that with that hair she might be untameable and be more trouble than 100 camels.

No, this definitely wasn't Bournemouth, even less was it similar when our train arrived and we fought our way onto it. However nobody travelled on the roof and so far I'd not seen anybody doing so.

Chapter 14

Gardens, Shopping and Sightseeing

Simon said, "You can take over the garden, tell the Mali just what you want."

I had long since given up the idea that what goes on in the garden is just what I want. There are reasons for this, firstly we never have a common language, I have no Hindi, the Mali nods and smiles and that's the end of the matter, he continues to do just what he intended to do in the first place for, secondly, our ideas differ and the regimented straight lines were the same here as in Pakistan. Even when I eventually left there were still things that I should have liked to be done. I'd tried one or two demonstrations of block planting to no avail, later though the straight rows didn't seem obvious as the flowers bloomed and the garden became a mass of colour.

"Are there garden centres?" I asked Simon.

"They're called nurseries here, Thompson will know and drive you to them," replied Simon. Thompson did know and we spent some delightful times buying plants for very little that back home would have cost a fortune. I bought a banana tree for twenty-five rupees (£1 = 65r). I also bought a good looking small fork and trowel for the Mali's tool looked crude and inefficient, he smiled delightedly but continued to use his own, doing all the garden operations with it. I expect my tools are still sitting there awaiting my return. I couldn't win on my group plant arrangements either, next day they would all be back in rows.

Hari too liked things indoors in straight lines or at right angles to each other so that the sitting room always had a geometrical look to it in the morning which soon changed once the family were home and in occupation.

Minju was an excellent cook, she was short and well upholstered, she was always laughing though I had the feeling that she kept Hari and her family well under control. She was immaculate and came every day in different and brilliant clothes. We went to market together and I was thankful in the labyrinth of passages to see her bright purple, pink or blue garments just ahead of me. I could follow her chubby cheerful figure round the stalls, and enjoy the spices, vegetables and the seemingly endless variety of merchandise without the worry of getting lost. One sight I enjoyed was the fish filleting on a huge upright knife which looked exceedingly dangerous. Minju loved the marketing part of her job and I think she probably paid half of what I should have been asked. While examining a fish an ugly looking brute, I was convinced that one bit me and I had a poisoned thumb.

"How could a dead fish bite you?" exclaimed Peter disbelievingly.

"Well it did and I have this thumb to show for it. I shall bring plastic gloves next time."

I loved these flourishing markets although the wet dirty passages were a great contrast to the beauty of the arranged vegetable stalls.

It's the contrasts in Delhi that hit me most and must make everybody think and ask why. There are the horrible refuse heaps, the overcrowded rusty dirty rag-made conglomeration of shacks with its inhabitants who, in their poverty, beg by the roadside or turn over the garbage. Compare this with the Delhi designed by Lutyens with clean wide open spaces and gardens, broad roads, generously built houses, bungalows and a feeling of space. It seems like two different cities, each almost unaware of the other, I suppose it is all part of the bewildering vastness that is Delhi.

Driving here seems to bear little relationship to driving back home. I assume there must be rules here but if there are everyone ignores them - it's each for himself and may the biggest win. No-one crosses at the right place and even if they do no-one stops for them. Beggars wander in and out of the traffic jungle and hope to catch you at the traffic lights, some are hopefully flogging toys, papers, tissues and other oddments which they push through a foolishly left open window. It's hazardous. The sacred cow is safe though, no-one dare run over one of these odd looking beasts.

Somebody once said to me that he found Delhi 'uninteresting'. I take little notice of other people's opinions, particularly in relation to travel, but I suppose that if all you do is drive round the overloaded and polluted roads there is little of interest except the total lack of rules and the sacred cows placidly chewing the cud on a zebra crossing. I found so much to see in Delhi and a good guide book will say the same. I'd seen very little on my last short visit, this time I wanted to find some of the old cities as well as see something of Old Delhi.

The family had not been so very long here and their time had been taken up in house hunting, school visiting and generally fitting up and settling down. They now welcomed a bit of exploration and I was not left entirely in the care of Thompson. He, however, was a great help in finding the post office, banks and guiding me around the complex interlaced alleyways of the walled Old Delhi. He guarded me too from the very persistent street traders.

"I am knowing Delhi very well and I am looking after you," he told me proudly as he waved away some over determined seller. He did know Delhi well and always knew the quickest way around the streets to any of the places we were visiting.

We took a picnic to Tughlaqabad which was the third city, the others walked, explaining that it was not far 'through the park'. I am not so sure of my outer Delhi geography that I could myself lead anyone through this park but everyone arrived jauntily so it cannot have been too far. I am not so sure either of the history of this area to be able to explain the sequence of the various cities. Tughlaqabad is a vast place with massive walls, now a complete ruin.

Tughla's tomb is across the road and there were monkeys everywhere here.

The Qutab Minar was another place we visited, I was anxious to see this amazing building but also to see the famous iron post, said to be so pure it never rusts.

"If you can put your arms around it backwards …," began Peter but never finished as the post had a fence around it, perhaps too many people had back problems attempting this. I forgot to ask what happened if the feat was successful.

The shops were exciting to me and Connaught Place with its circular layout was a wonderful place to look for Christmas gifts.

Chapter 15

Goa

"If we stay here for Christmas," said Jennie to Simon, "you'll keep on working and working, the phone will be endlessly ringing and … "

Simon, interrupting her, dropped his bombshell with, "I've managed to get us all into a hotel in Goa for Christmas." He said it in a casual, bored sort of voice as if he did it every day. In the appreciative ensuing silence there has to be a dissenting voice.

"I'd rather have Christmas here," muttered Peter, perhaps objections have to be raised by the young. He was ignored, of course, while the rest of us considered the scheme. I felt a certain amount of sympathy towards him for Christmas here would have had, for me, a quiet charm but then who could seriously complain about sun and sand? Delhi was now home to me and I knew little about Goa. Wasn't it said to be touristy now and weren't there other places on India's great coastline that we might prefer?

It was booked and settled and now we had the task of getting ourselves there, or rather, Jennie had this task and it needed much organisation and patience. Christmas is a busy time and all flights were booked. On hearing of our plans old friends decided to join us, John from Pakistan with his new and to us, as yet unknown girlfriend Kim. From Nepal Ann and Patrick also needed a sun and sand break, and from the cold of England, Gill had been invited by Liz and had her parents' permission to come. It was to be quite a party and Jennie had all the travel arrangements to make for ten of us. John's friend, Kim, was making her own way from America.

Liz seemed to have told many of her friends to be there, that is if I interpreted the many phone calls correctly, some even turned up but their travel arrangements were not our problem.

I looked up Goa on the map and found it to be a tiny state, only part of India since the 1960's, small, that is compared with the areas of the other states, situated on the south-west coast, it was Portuguese for many years.

The travel agents were half-hearted, "Yes, there is a train," they told us, "and maybe it will be having seats on it."

I pointed out that I needed more than a seat if I was to be travelling all night, John too had sounded delicate, coming from Afghanistan, he had had flu and was badly in need of rest. The allocation of seats on the train seemed a hit and miss affair and so we shouldn't know until the last minute, "But we will try," said the travel agent girl brightly. "Or," she added, "we could find a flight to Mumbai and then a boat."

No-one seemed keen on the boat idea, it was a coast hugging catamaran and took even longer than the train, I thought it sounded fun but I only had sour looks when I suggested we gave it a try.

The railway line from Bombay to Goa had not been finished, so even if we arrived safely in Bombay (I must remember to call it Mumbai) we still had not finished our journey. "Isn't there a flight," asked Jennie, beginning to tire of the whole undertaking.

"Oh yes," replied the girl as if to the mentally incapable, or were we only eccentric?

Surprisingly the train tickets with berths for ten came through, perhaps it was more simple than it appeared, the flight onward to Panjim in Goa was booked and we were mentally on our way.

We all collected in Delhi and we would pick Kim up in Mumbai, it was to be an early start. We were all looking forward to it not only as a holiday of a lifetime but as medicine for we all had Delhi coughs and Ann, coming from Katmandu, said that pollution was even worse there, her cough sounded the worst of the lot. I refused an invitation to go back to Nepal with them, I don't like to refuse such invitations but pollution worse than Delhi sounded uninviting. Now all that sun and warmth would cure us all of our ills. Everyone in Delhi said it was a bad winter, it was not cold by our standards, the endless smog must be the cough maker and everyone seemed to be hacking, scraping and spitting.

Delhi railway station needs a whole chapter on its own, several books perhaps if all the histories and intertwining stories of the hundreds of people collected there were to be told. There are all the pushing, jostling crowds and the sleeping bodies (are they only sleeping?), bundles wrapped in blankets and other piles of strange belongings all gathered here. Are they and their possessions all travelling, are they waiting for trains or just living here? I had thought our luggage looked a motley assortment, it was nothing compared with this collection. We arrived in two cars and were immediately set upon by the porters, there appeared to be countless numbers of these but Simon organised only six for our needs. These porters must be registered for they wear red shirts and have a numbered armband. I blindly followed my luggage remembering the porter's number as I went. One cheerful note is that these porters do know where they're going and there were ten of us to board our own carriage on the Bombay express. A struggle but eventually we seemed to be organised into our compartments, they were a pleasant surprise and a comfortable journey looked hopeful. Our porters then stood over us negotiating for their payment, our luggage looked enough for an expedition to unknown and uncivilised parts for an indefinite time, Patrick has his paragliding gear, Simon a very large cold box (we were later very grateful for the contents) and everyone else the usual collection of I-might-need-it oddments. We were told that as luggage goes with you 'only take a small bag'. No-one had taken much notice of this nor by the look of all their paraphernalia had any of the other passengers. The whole world seemed to be travelling on the Bombay Express. This was a 'proper' train, there was no hanging out of doors on this one. The train didn't seem over-full, what had happened to that great wave of pushing, shoving humanity? Most seemed to be left behind on the platform.

It was a good journey, food was served at regular intervals, stops revealed deserted darkened stations, it was all very mysterious. I slept well on a bottom bunk and all the others were still asleep when breakfast was served, I remember eating several of these, at least three omelettes and downing several thermoses of tea. I was ready for anything.

Our arrival in Bombay seemed a surprise to everyone, someone was asking about breakfast and I didn't like to admit that most of it was inside me.

I forgot who said "Never eat on trains in India," but I do remember Simon saying "Delhi belly is a matter of luck." I think he's right for often those who suffer have done all the right things and those, and I am among them, (touch wood) who do all the wrong things like eating on trains, manage to avoid such tummy troubles.

There was general panic as the train drew into the station and most of our party were still struggling out of their bunks, everyone hustled everyone else as we hastily gathered up our belongings and happily realised that the cool box was considerably lighter.

The station, as at Delhi, was a scrambling mass of people but we were leaving it behind us, not entering it and we were glad to follow the porters to find reliable taxis.

We were to pick up Kim in her hotel but by the time we arrived the family were clamouring for breakfast, fortunately the fact that I didn't want any passed unnoticed, I preferred to take advantage of Kim's offer of her 'facilities' to have a refreshing shower and remove traces of the general grubbiness of the train.

The next stage on this journey was to the airport and a short flight to Panjim in Goa. Panjim is the capital of this small state and when we passed through it I had the impression of a pleasant small town. The airport appeared to be unfinished or was it just disorganised but like most visitors to Goa, we were on our way to the beaches, this was the last stage of our journey. The countryside looked all it was cracked up to be with palm trees, bougainvillaea, warm sea breezes and all the atmosphere that is expected in the tropics. We breathed deeply and started to shed clothes.

"You'll find the hotel a bit basic," said Simon, "but we can eat out at all those wonderful places you hear about and it's a nice quiet place." No-one took this last remark too seriously, fortunately, as he had no idea having booked on the recommendation of a friend, or was it a rumour?

Yes, the hotel was a bit basic, our party took up quite a bit of it but who, in a place like Goa, wants to stay in a bedroom anyway and the eating areas were outside roofed rooms, it looked fine to me. The small twin-bedded rooms had concrete floors with a mat, 2 chairs and a table, the 'facilities' looked adequate. I had a room to myself as our party, now eleven, was an odd number. There appeared to be a leak in the shower room and after I had paddled about in it for a while I decided it didn't matter, I prefer a bit of basicality if there is too much pomp and ostentation I begin to worry about how much money is going on frills and unnecessary trifles. Simon put his head round the door and told me to stop messing about as we were going out for a meal.

"What's wrong with here?" I asked.

"We've got to try all those wonderful fish restaurants," he replied.

The meal was very unsatisfactory, perhaps we chose the wrong place, we returned to our own hotel. I was quite happy to settle here after all we were here for the beaches, the warmth and the fresh air.

It was very warm in my room but there was a fan (or punkah) and I turned this on. It didn't work so I went in search of the management, this was a good move as it brought an instant response from the many inhabitants, maybe they were the hotel staff or the family or both, the room became crowded with some mending, trying to mend, holding things, giving helpful advice or just watching and bringing tea.

I yawned hopefully once or twice and everyone said cheerfully that I must be tired.

Simon arrived and asked why I wasn't in bed as all the others were just going.

He looked at the happy assembly, "Have you another room?" he asked Bromley, the hotel owner.

"Oh yes, the one next door is empty," replied Bromley brightly.

"I wonder ..." I began but there was no need to ask, everyone grabbed my belongings and I was nearly bodily removed. Thankfully I went to bed and I was already comfortably settled when I discovered that the lights didn't work. I closed my eyes, after all I had a torch.

I woke early and looking round decided I didn't like my new room, except for the plumbing it wasn't identical and there was no table. I still had the keys to my old room, there wasn't a soul to be seen so I tried the fan which worked and moved myself back, I felt it was meant to be mine.

The early mornings here were wonderful, there was an outside sunbed and my early rising was soon discovered. Tea was always brought to me here either by Bromley himself or one of his staff. One of these would peep round the wall of our block and seeing me would rush back to put the kettle on. These people had their priorities right. I'd had a brief look around the kitchen, it was beautifully clean and I decided that I liked this place. In retrospect I still do and would heartily recommend it, there was a relaxed atmosphere mixed with friendly kindness. I had more meals here than the others who went in search of the supposed fantastic delights of Goa. I was never impressed, my first meal had been disappointing - a prawn cocktail with very few prawns and a revolting sauce - and I wondered what had happened to the marvellous cuisine we had heard about. We found this deterioration at many places, we were told there were 'too many tourists, too much advertising - market forces you understand'. The prices too had gone up. I had some of my favourite meals at our simple hotel where Bromley's wife Beate looked after me, it was a family place with kindly family helpfulness.

One of the noticeable things about Goa is that it is so easy going, it's a subtle thing this, and not easy to describe. The descriptive bits are easy, all the expected delights, the long sandy beaches, waves breaking on a beautiful shore, palm trees galore. It's the no hurry relaxed atmosphere that I enjoyed as it's just right for the holiday mood. A waiter or a workman or whoever happened to be around would lean on a convenient wall for ages discussing the merits of an omelette or scrambled eggs. These people seemed contented with their lot, perhaps they should be with such a country to live in. Perhaps the growth of tourism will spoil all this, perhaps it depends on the tourist.

There was a beach not far away but we were disappointed to find that the shacks which were supposed to supply the needs of the tourists and were mentioned in the guide books as typical of the beaches, were no longer there. "Unhygienic," the hotels told us. Possibly this was true, certainly the inhabitants didn't seem worried as to where they performed their natural functions.

"It's fairly shitty," said Liz who doesn't believe in mincing her words. It's such a pity too. That there is so much rubbish, plastic bags, tins as well as dogs and cows, although these may have a use as scavengers.

We had come to enjoy ourselves and a bit of muck wasn't going to put us off. It was an interesting beach as it seemed to cater for different cultures along its length. At one end anything on or nothing on appeared to be the order of the day, the middle bit was fairly normal and at the end where the Indians collected swimming fully clothed seemed to be the norm. I walked the length of the beach and wondered if the Indians were right and the bellies and buttocks (not to mention the boobs) would perhaps be better covered. It grew hot and I returned to the comparative coolness of the hotel.

"I think," said Simon, following me soon afterwards, "that we ought to hire a motor scooter, we could see more." Simon too doesn't lie on beaches for very long, whispering palms are great for a while. "I thought you were going to walk," I said, rather nastily.

"We're going to walk tomorrow," he said defensively, "but you others could do with wheels."

"Bromley will know how to hire one," I said seeing our host hovering in the background. Bromley did know of course, and this scooter hiring turned out to be another social pastime, all sorts of scooters arrived with their owners and followers. One wasn't going to be enough. Liz fancied the idea, Adam too looked hopeful. Patrick thought he might have one, John didn't want to be left out. Only Peter and I, one too young and one no longer so sure of her ability, didn't add to the excited interest as he and I quietly assured each other that we should be quite safe on the pillions.

Simon and Patrick looked the scooters over. "Has this any brakes?" asked Simon, after viewing a particularly shaky looking vehicle. The 'very good brakes' proved to be non-existent and a doubtful method of stopping using the feet didn't appeal.

"Whose is it?" brought forth such a complicated list of possible owners that Simon thought it unwise to get involved. By this time Liz had practically commandeered a very pretty blue one, Adam was looking longingly at a slightly more powerful black model on the pillion of which Peter was firmly perched and Patrick was already paying up. Eventually everyone was satisfied with Liz and Adam ready to drive off. John was more cautious but he too was suited and with

Kim on the back prepared to see something of the countryside.

"Petrol," shouted Simon, still handing out money for hire but no-one listened. It was only John who later ran out and had to abandon his bike under a tree.

"Where is it?" asked Simon when John and Kim arrived in a taxi.

"Under a tree," replied John.

"Which tree?" we all asked.

John seemed doubtful and his description of a tree unhelpful.

"Better keep the taxi, maybe he'll know," suggested Simon.

We all set off, some of us in the taxi and all shouting different directions to the driver who, poor man, was so confused that he was probably driving in the opposite direction. It was Adam on his own scooter who found it.

"Where?" asked Simon.

"Under a tree," replied Adam. There was a silence. Adam added, "I'll take you to it," he said to John with quiet confidence. He takes after his Grandfather.

There did not appear to be many rules and regulations for the riders of these machines, perhaps if there is trouble a buying out system is in order, no helmets seemed to be worn, no limit on the number of people piled on to them. Taxes? Licences? Or was it a free for all, the youngsters were told to be careful and rode off. Please don't quote me.

We could now go further afield, see other beaches and some of the countryside. After a few days the party broke up into smaller groups, the young people finding friends of their own age, Patrick went paragliding accompanied by a worried Ann, John and Kim were content in each other's company. Simon and Jennie were still determined to walk the coast; that left me. I walked when I could but when it became too hot I took a taxi, this driver attached himself to

me in what looked like being a permanent relationship. If
he lost me for a minute he came looking for me.

"He's too fussy," said Simon, "can't you get rid of him?"

"He's useful," I replied.

"You could use him to take you to some of the stages of
our walks," said Simon. "We can meet you at various places,
you can go inland or to the ferries."

This plan worked remarkably well and I am sure I saw
much more of the wonderful countryside than anyone else.
The only snag was the taxi driver who worried every time
we had to wait. Where was his Goan philosophy? By good
luck or good management we always met up at the appointed
place so even this driver started to enjoy himself. I had
never seen anything funny in this arrangement and it was
not until I noticed that he always joined a group, told a
story with much laughter all round, that I began to see the
joke. Why hire a taxi and then walk? I caught the word
'Mummy' and could see something of why it was thought
so funny. They all looked over at me sitting sedately in the
taxi but I had my own back on the driver for if I wandered
away for any length of time he started to worry again and
became quite distressed. I couldn't think why for he knew
where we started from and could always return me or maybe
he thought he wouldn't get paid if he lost me. The ferries
were fun, everyone pushed on and we reached the opposite
bank often without mishap, sometimes the tide took us too
far downstream but amid much shouting and speculation,
the right spot was reached. I enjoyed these trips enormously
but my favourite of all was Terekmol fort in the far north on
a tiny region beyond the Terekmol river. This river was one
we crossed by ferry. The fort now housed a hotel and there
was also a church in the courtyard. The views from the
battlements were magnificent, it was easy to see why such a
site was chosen for a fort. I'd like to stay there, it looked

different. On this particular walk we all went home in the taxi, this made the driver happy and he turned up again next morning in a more relaxed mood.

We decided on Old Goa for the day's trip. "It's one of the musts," said Simon. We added another taxi from the rank of hopefuls waiting for clients, there were eight of us. I wasn't sure what we were going to see in Old Goa, one of our party had a guide book which showed pictures of magnificent buildings whereas I was expecting something more like Old Mombassa. Some of these fine churches are still in use but most of this remarkable city has disappeared into the ever encroaching jungle, lost, hidden and almost forgotten. It was this part I found so fascinating and felt that a one-day outing was inadequate for the exploration it needed. It was cool inside the lofty churches and cathedrals but the jungle looked inviting too. No-one seemed interested in the overgrown ruins, the crowds were in the preserved buildings. It is in the overgrown parts that the realisation dawns of the vastness of the abandoned city that once thrived here. There had been a great port here too, large ships had come up the river with cargoes of silks and spices, china and even horses. Now the river front was that and no more, the busy port was only a memory where once these tall sailing ships would have docked. There was mystery and romance here in imagining the once bustling working city.

Old Goa Ruins

What had happened and why, I wondered? This city in the early part of the sixteenth century was called the 'Rome of the East', it had grown rapidly with Portuguese trading wealth. Disease helped in its destruction, cholera struck several times and malaria was rife. Too soon the growth of a fertile land overwhelmed deserted buildings.

If any of my readers should find themselves in Goa may I ask them not to spend all the time lying on a beach but to explore this fascinating place and particularly to find this hidden city. I am not a historian but I find it thought provoking to view such a curious and once lived in place and to wonder about the happenings there.

The crowds these days are sight-seers and the trading mostly souvenir sellers, we came upon many of these as we went in search of our taxis. Someone had locked a large gate and only a narrow turnstile was available for the masses to pass through, it was unbelievable chaos, it was a great contrast from this pushing and heat when we arrived in the cool overgrown ruins.

We ended the day by driving to another fort with a hotel, it was the sort of place where you hastily smooth your hair, pull your skirt down a bit and think hastily about your bank balance.

We ate here and most of the party walked home along the beach in the moonlight. I was not among them, after all why walk when there is a waiting taxi?

The removed shacks had been useful to tourists, there were still one or two that had been left unmolested, perhaps they had passed the fitness test. After being on a beach all morning we were all needing refreshment. There was a large tented structure at the back of the beach where I had been resting under a boat.

"What's that, is that a café, can we get drinks there?" I asked Liz.

"I need more than a drink," said Peter.

"That's a great place," said Liz, who by now had a good working knowledge of the various eating places, "It's very laid back," she added.

"Let's try it," suggested Jennie, not quite sure of the 'laid back' bit.

There were no tables and chairs, customers were either sitting cross-legged or lying about on mats, they all looked very smug or just dopey and fuddled. The letters R.I.E. were hung up, could this be 'Rest in Ecstasy', I felt sure it was. Straw matting also hung on the walls along with netting and a large picture of a duck.

An attempt had been made to make the place look African with a huge black face hung with lovelocks but no-one in the place looked remotely African except for one white youth whose matted hairstyle looked dirty rather than authentic. Africans believe in cleanliness.

We sat round a six inch high table and tried to assume expressions to show we were part of the scene. Poor Lizzie, she must have felt embarrassment for her orthodox family, or are we? It can't be normal to take along your Grandmother. There was a peculiar smell, the girl sitting on my left was smoking something and whatever it was, it wasn't doing her any good at all, I hoped she wouldn't be sick on me, I decided to move where a post would support my back, being cross-legged doesn't suit me any more.

No-one could say that this wasn't a 'nice little open air café', it was all there, fresh air, sand, sea, sun and swaying palm trees. Peter looked round the tent and inspired by the success of his remark in Pakistan he turned to Liz and asked, "Do you come here often?"

Eventually a young man strolled over and presented a dirty card that served as a menu, he sat on his haunches and grinned and giggled all the time, perhaps, Adam suggested, because he had no intention of fulfilling the orders given him. I asked for cheese on toast and at this he laughed outright and no wonder for, when it did arrive an hour later, it was a minute stale bun to which a lump of cheese had been cemented. Before this a cold coffee was brought to Adam but the others were still waiting when I left to see if I could find an 'unlaidback' place where coffee was served quickly and hot. I felt sure I had seen such a place a short way up the road, it also had chairs. Jennie joined me as I was drinking an excellent cup quickly served.

"I don't mind a place being laid back," she said, "as long as it doesn't extend to the waiters."

"Two minutes for a coffee," I said, "would you like one?"

Another café was, according to Simon, "On the other side."

"The other side of what," I asked.

"Of the estuary, it's quite narrow, just a little stream, you could wade it, it's only knee deep."

It was dusk and I was expecting a quiet little supper in our own hotel where I was often the only guest eating, it was simple and I liked it. This particular evening Simon wouldn't hear of it.

"Everyone's going over," he said, "It's a good place."

Wading an unknown estuary in the dark didn't appeal to me even if it was only knee deep.

Patrick joined in, "There's a bridge," he said, "but it's a long way round."

This would mean a pillion ride, surely better than wading. Mention of a bridge struck a chord. Was this the bridge I'd read about, described as the ugliest bridge in the world?

"I want to see that bridge," I said.

"Climb on the back," said Simon, "We'll go and look at it."

It was a rough road, if road there was which I doubted, but there was certainly a bridge. This massive concrete structure loomed out at us, its menacing bulk undoubtedly living up to its reputation. How could anyone have built such a monstrosity, unless there was an overload of concrete that had to be used up? The track curved suddenly to go through this tunnel, water had been lapping on both sides of us and occasionally trees showed up in the bike lights when appeared to be right in our path. On the other side I could now see the 'little stream'. Not wide by Indian standards, just about the width of the Thames and tidal.

"It looks daunting," I said, "I'm glad I didn't attempt it."

Simon gave me one of his looks of where-is-your-pioneering-spirit? All the others were at the café, bone dry too, for no-one seemed to have waded.

Next day I examined the estuary in full daylight and with sun shining, I could see a delightful small deserted beach. With a low tide and by the mouth of the river it did indeed look wadeable. The young people soon splashed happily through it and I wasn't going to be left behind, there were rocks giving shade and inviting looking pools. "Only knee deep," I told myself but halfway across and already up to my waist I nearly turned back but by then I could see Liz and Gill claiming the best places and I persevered, after all my clothes would soon dry in the sun. My swimming costume was already dry, it was in a knapsack on my back. Some Indian ladies, well-covered with all their garments, seeing me arrive safely, decided to try their luck and follow me. They soon turned back with terrified cries even though spurred on by their men folk. The little beach was worth it, it was well washed and clean and we had it to ourselves.

In October, when I left England, Christmas was well on its way. In Delhi just before Christmas I heard someone ask an assistant in a big store, "Why are you decorating?"

"For Christmas," came the reply.

"Christmas? When is Christmas?"

(Now in Goa with a higher percentage of Christians than in the rest of India there seemed little sign of our October preparations. Sometimes this is earlier still for as I write, in August, I have already had three Christmas catalogues.)

On Christmas Eve and only then did the festivities begin, to me this seemed the right time and the excitement with decorations, cribs being built, stars shining and carols sung, was infectious. We all joined in, it was a time full of life and in the morning bells rant out, music boomed, horns tooted and dogs howled like wolves. "I shan't get morning tea today." I told myself but there it was with a lovely rose to brighten the tray. If only 30% of Goans are Christians the other 60% could hardly keep out of it. The family rose earlier than usual.

"Not quite like home," said Peter, "but very good all the same. Can we have scrambled eggs for breakfast?"

I needed a haircut and went to look for a hairdresser, could there be somewhere, other than expensive hotel boutiques, with someone able to cut hair that seemed overlong in the heat of Goa. It seemed an unlikely place to look among all the touristy shops and shacks that bordered the narrow road. Tucked between two of these shacks I found 'Annettes Beauty Parlour' and there was probably Annette herself leaning on a post outside her establishment. She didn't appear to have a great deal of business.

"Do you cut hair?" I asked. She stopped chewing and looked delighted as she ushered me into her surprisingly clean little room. She charged me twenty-five rupees. The exchange rate was sixty-five to the pound, I felt guilty when I gave her fifty for it wasn't a bad cut and it was less than the tip I would expect to give back home. Adam was so impressed when I arrived back at the hotel that he immediately set out to find a barber and returned with a neatly shaved head.

"It was getting in my eyes," he said, "do you like it?"

"It's a sensation," I replied.

It was sometime before it dawned on me what a dolphin boat was, obvious, of course, when one thinks about it. On the day it was announced that we were all going on it the penny dropped and I realised that we were going to see the dolphins! It was a lovely day with a canopied boat and there were plenty of dolphins. The coastline was always in view and this, along with the dolphins playing all around us, made it a first rate trip. It's a wonderful coastline and best viewed from the sea.

I love boats and the idea of going to market by boat appealed to both Jennie and myself.

"It's the Anjuna Flea Market today," shouted Liz as the young people prepared to set off there on their bikes. Jennie looked interested, "You and Joy can go by boat," Liz told her.

We found the boats on the shore, most seemed to be going to the market so we had plenty of choice, we found one we liked, it filled up and we landed on Anjuna beach. The rest of the party were already there and were having bits of themselves painted with black henna, there were beautiful patterns and I thought it an interesting form of art but, in spite of being told that it washed off, I resisted an offer from Kim to be adorned myself. Kim had a natty little pattern in an alluring front position.

This market was fun, stalls were all over the beach and under the trees, it was full of goods of all sorts with plenty of Kashmiri and Tibetan traders, these had jewellery, ethnic crafts and textiles, I bought all my home-going gifts at very reasonable prices, Liz helped me bargain, she was, and is, good at this, almost embarrassingly so. I should give in long before she does. Everyone was friendly and the food was fine. It was a great day out.

Some memories of Goa will always stay with me - the sleek cats in the fish restaurant and the spinach soup Jennie and I ordered.

"This isn't spinach soup," said Jennie, "it's chicken soup."

"It's spinach soup," insisted the waiter.

"It's got bits of white stuff in it!"

"That's potato."

"So it's potato and chicken soup?"

"It's spinach soup," argued the waiter, pointing to a minute green speck.

"Potato and chicken with tiny bits of spinach," I now joined the discussion and started to poke my own tiny scraps of green around my bowl.

"Take it away," said Jennie.

Lastly on our final night I had the bright idea of changing beds and I had a wonderful sand-free night.

Chapter 16

Festivals and Jaunts

"We've been invited to a barbecue at the Farms," said Simon shortly after our return to Delhi.

"What farms?" I asked, for I was not sure what this entailed.

"The houses are outside the town," put in Jennie, and I wasn't very much the wiser. Nor was I sure where we were going but I found it interesting when we arrived. These houses appear to have been built on grand or no longer grand feudal estates. That's the impression I had from the big fancy gates and the high overgrown walls. Within these compounds are good sized modern houses and, better still, ground enough for a swimming pool, tennis court, croquet pitch, (was it a pitch, the boys were playing football on it?) Added to this was a sizeable vegetable patch and a shady woodland walk. It was wonderfully peaceful with fresh clean air.

"Why can't we live out here?" asked Peter, a keen sportsman.

"Too far out," replied Simon, "too many of us all doing different things, but perhaps..." I felt sure that he was attracted to the idea and Jennie, too, was breathing deeply. As I walked round enjoying the trees and the flourishing garden I too would have been tempted.

On the way home we came through a district of garden nurseries. We stopped at one of these to pick up a few plants that Simon felt would enhance their own Delhi patch. This was being improved day by day although the banana tree didn't look as if it would bear fruit in my day. The grass began to look like a lawn and trees, climbers and shrubs flourished. Winter, such as it was, was suddenly over, spring approached, the dreaded season was summer when everything shrank in the heat and dust.

I must mention another festival called 'Holi'. This seemed to consist mainly of paint throwing so I never positively found out what we were celebrating.

"If you are sensible," I was told, "stay indoors."

"It's gruesome," said Peter as he came into the house with green and purple water paint dripping off him from head to foot.

"Weird," added Adam, following Peter and covered in a nasty orange-pink mixture and carrying a very large water cylinder which was the instrument for inflicting this mess.

"I am not liking," said Hari, shaking his head as two more boys followed, equally equipped and equally coloured. All drifted down to the shower room.

"Not like, not like," moaned Minju, wringing her hands, "house clean, not like!"

House no longer clean I had to admit as I viewed the trail of paint through hall and downstairs. The boys were all in old clothes but the shower room … Poor Hari.

I was becoming quite an old hand at sight-seeing but I hesitated when a friend of Jennie's said, "Could you take Uncle Guthrie with you if you are going to the Taj Mahal?" Perhaps she mistook my hesitation for consent as she continued undaunted by my silence.

"You were getting on well with him at supper last night, as you know it's his first time in India and he's longing to go, I'd go myself but I can't get away in term-time."

I wasn't going to the Taj Mahal, I'd been once before and didn't particularly want to go again, it's a 'once in a lifetime' visit and marble tombs, although interesting the first time, don't compel me to go again.

However - "He says he'll pay all expenses," said this friend, "he wants to go on the train, can you arrange it?"

The train, now that was a different story, and I agreed to make all the arrangements and to accompany Guthrie on this trip, for who could resist a free day out with a quiet companion and Uncle Guthrie was not a touristy type, more of an Oxford don academic type. Given good weather I should enjoy myself.

I felt flattered at the trust in me, and a little guilty when all I had to do was to visit the travel agent who had organised us across India. The guide book suggested buying a timetable of trains but I felt that only a travel agent or someone with years of experience would be able to understand the intricacies of Indian rail travel. Thompson took me to our travel agent next morning for I felt that the small percentage added to the expense would be well worthwhile. A travel agent will make your decisions for you, arrange taxi and guide, hand over the tickets, tell you how very comfortable you will be and leave you to get on with it.

It was all so easy, and I tried to look confident as if I arranged this sort of thing every day, Guthrie obviously thought I did and looked at me in a very positive and secure way. I felt it couldn't go wrong and strangely enough it didn't. Our train seats were numbered and booked, we arrived at Agra to find a taxi waiting for us with Guthrie's name held high. This took us to a hotel for coffee and a wash and brush up (breakfast was served on the train and included in the fare). I had booked to 'do' everything for Guthrie who not only wanted to see the Taj Mahal but the Agra fort, the baby Taj and one other with deer and monkeys, on my last short visit we had only briefly visited the Taj so I was glad to see all these places at someone else's expense. This second time round I had time to admire the wonderful inlaid work on the tomb and to admire the warm red sandstone of surrounding buildings which are such a contrast to the white marble. The inlaid work of semi-precious stones is so beautiful but showing signs of deterioration, sad this, and very difficult and expensive to maintain. I learned many things from our guide that I hadn't bothered to find out for myself from sheer laziness, having a guide who was determined to give us our money's worth was no bad thing for now I heard all sorts of facts such as the name of the lady for whom the tomb was built. She was called Mumtaz and the monument took twenty-two years to build. I hoped no-one ever puts up such a tombstone to me, this is very unlikely and Mumtaz had fourteen children in seventeen years of marriage so perhaps she deserved it. We shall never know what her reaction would have been.

I am still vague about Mughal history but I learnt how to tell a Mughal garden because it is divided into four parts and the Mughal Emperor who built the Taj Mahal was called Shah Jahan and he was deposed by his son, imprisoned in the fort and spent the rest of his life there. We went to the fort and found that there was a very good view of the Taj Mahal from there so he could always look across and think about her. It didn't look to me to be a bad place to be imprisoned but then I know little about the conditions of the time. Shah Jahan had always meant to build a replica of the Taj in black for himself but he never got round to it. I suppose it would all have been good for the building trade.

I learned that the river was the Yamuna, there seemed to be plenty of water in it.

Although usually I am against trailing round with a guide, I have to admit that I have met some who are amusing and helpful, this one was determined that we should see everything and sometime monotonously boring. In spite of this he was a lively companion and when side-tracked from his memorised recital could be interesting and entertaining, his high pitched lecture forgotten he talked in a normal voice. We collected a small guide-less group but he was having none of it and stopped talking until they had gone. We had paid him, we were his and he was ours alone.

There were so many people, many, many more than on my last visit with Simon; the open garden layout would be quite spoilt by wire surrounds but the crowds pushing by nearly sent the people in front into a pool. I grabbed one woman and Guthrie grabbed her companion and we saved the wet outcome, the water is shallow but the woman's glittering, flowing draperies would have been ruined and the commotion, caused by her distress, profuse.

We were told there is no longer visiting by moonlight. I wondered why, but perhaps with so many visitors it is difficult to guard all the semi-precious objects. I hope I am not slandering these visitors as another possible reason could be the need to reduce the pollution, evidence of which may be seen quite clearly. The travel agents do not mention either the pollution or the fixed hours and 'not opening on Monday'.

We didn't manage to visit the Fatehpur Sikri. Jennie said she thought we should not have missed it so I could still go again if someone else dishes up a generous uncle.

"Joy organised it so well," I heard Uncle Guthrie tell his niece, "it was well worth the small outlay, an excellent outing and we saw so much."

'Small outlay' was a serious fortune to me and I glowed happily as I listened to this praise.

Guthrie never knew how easy it had been and if his niece suspected she didn't let on, she looked hopeful when we said we might visit the Red Fort, a possibility we had discussed on the train return journey, maybe she felt that a bachelor uncle might later be a liability but, although we got on well as tourists, I had no intention of renewing the friendship back home.

Thompson took us to the Red Fort, this is another of Shah Jahan's buildings, at one time there was a moat surrounding the fort but it is now empty of water, I was glad we had Thompson who kept off would-be guides and touts, there are shops at the fort entrance and the building itself, as its name suggests, is made of the warm sandstone. There is a throne to see but I thought Guthrie was under the impression that he was being propositioned when a scruffy guide offered to show him the ladies bathroom. Thompson explained that this was a showpiece at the fort.

Guthrie returned home after his short visit well pleased with his trip but I was surprised when a friend of Simon's asked me, "Would you take my parents up to Shimla next year when they come, they want to go on that train as well as see the town."

I opened my mouth to protest but changed my mind.

"Of course," I said with pleasant thoughts of next year in my mind and wondering if I could now set up as a world guide or even a travel agent. "Perhaps not," I told myself for an Indian railway guide would defeat me.

"Shall you go to the Surajkund Mela?" asked Patience, a much valued friend.

"Tell me more," I replied.

By then I thought I knew what to expect at a mela but this one was quite something. A mela had been described to be as 'a sort of fete' by someone else as 'a sale of work' and by a third as 'a glorified car boot sale'. It was none of these, nothing like our village sale of work or the school fete and as to a car boot sale - words fail me.

"It's a big affair," said Patience who had been the year before, "it's beyond Tughaqabad, Thomson will know the way."

Thompson did know and was delighted to be going at our expense so we collected some more friends and set off.

I must quote from the local paper about this event:-

"This year the duration of the mela has been reduced by one day and it will get over by February 14th ... it promises to bring forth an unprecedented exposition of handlooms. It seeks to expose the visitors to one of the richest areas of the country with centuries old traditions of handlooms and handicrafts, dance and music ... enchanting cultural

programmes will be presented ... Nestled among Avavalli hills
sprawled over 26 acres of undulating land and situated at a
distance of just 8km from South Delhi, this mela provides an
authentic picture of rural India."

I am unhappy about the last statement, a 'picture' perhaps
painted in glorified and embellished colours, it bore little
resemblance to the rural India I had seen. Some beautiful
houses had been constructed - they were clean and empty,
not surrounded by unkempt children and dogs playing in
the mud. The dancing was beautiful and so was the music,
Patience and I watched a dance supposed to represent village
life, the costumes were colourful and the dancing graceful,
one aspect of the dance was truthful, Patience looked at
me, "Typical," she said, "the women are doing all the work
as usual." Water carrying is not always so elegant in the
paddy fields where the women are often drudges.

We were 'exposed' to more than this for it was here I saw
a levitation. I feel sure it was some sort of conjuring trick
and not a patch on Paul Daniels but that didn't seem to
matter. It was the atmosphere of magic here among the
trees in India and surrounded by Indians all watching this
strange scene, it didn't matter whether we believed it or
not.

There was so much more to see and buy, one of our
party looked as if she was stocking up household textiles
for years to come, most of us bought something. I bought a
bamboo pipe for Hari which I later regretted as he practised
playing at 5.00 am in the mornings, going onto the roof to
do so.

This mela is an annual event and now that I know about
it I shall be careful to arrange my stay next year to coincide
with this fascinating affair. I must be there.

Next year? My time here this year had come to an end, I said my 'goodbyes' again and think of all that I have seen and all that I have not. India is an immense and wonderful country and I have not seen even one hundredth part of it. I have tried to absorb some of the atmosphere but I know I am not part of it. Always there is something just over the horizon or up in the beautiful blue hills. I look and I marvel and wish I had endless travelling time, it is impossible in India and in other countries to see all there is to see. I am reminded of an American woman I met who was travelling in England.

"Where have you been?" I asked her.

"My dear, I've been just about everywhere and seen just about everything."

"Well done, for how long is your stay?"

"Three days," she replied.

Ah?! Three days! I tell myself that Britain is only a small island and she had visited my own village so what more could I ask.

I returned home, this was my first homecoming when there was no Tom to greet me and to listen to my adventures, no hot consoling cups of cocoa or even a double brandy. I had moved around restlessly but now I had a small cottage by the sea to go to and I was once more on my beloved beach. Winter in India was fine but summer there - NO. The family would spend some time in England when it became unbearably hot in Delhi. I had this to look forward to as well as hopes for another winter trip. I should like to visit Africa again, would this be easier from India? Back to saving again.

I get out my atlas.

The End - or is it?

Chapter 17

A Delhi Diary

As I was writing "The End" a postcard shot through the letter box, it came from Bharatpur and showed striking pictures of birds. "You'll love this place," Simon wrote "and we are definitely coming here again. The birds are wonderful, painted storks in thousands, nesting and breeding. It is supposed to be fabulous over winter with migration in full swing. Lovely walks and trails too, with knowledgeable guides."

No question here of not being invited.

"I had your card," I said when I next phoned, "it sounds wonderful." It had dawned on me that migration there meant the reverse of swallow departure before the cold of an English winter. The birds would be coming, not going. It is some years since I watched birds arriving in Africa, I hadn't quite forgotten.

"What's it like there?" Simon asked.

"Cold," I replied.

"Just right here, so when do you come?" He didn't wait for a reply.

"Have you been to Jaipur?" he now asked enthusiastically.

No, I have not yet visited Jaipur but at this point I decided to visit my travel agent and set the ball rolling for my own personal migration. There are other places in my mind too, such as the nature reserve known as Ranthambhore where it is possible sometimes to see a tiger - now getting rarer and rarer. It is incredible that this magnificent beast is being slaughtered because of man's ignorance and stupidity. Eating bits of Tiger or making ointment of other bits in the unproved belief that it does - what? Cures what? I have no idea, I am just appalled that it can be allowed to happen.

So I want to see a tiger before man wipes him out.

Liz told me that she was travelling with me. She had been working nearby in order to make enough money to 'travel'. Can it be possible that she doesn't realise that she has already done so but with her spending habits it is unlikely that her wealth will accumulate to any great extent and I suspect that Simon has offered to pay her fare if she 'looks after' her grandmother. Travelling in India is still fairly reasonable if one isn't too fussy and it is a big country of which she can't, as yet, have seen very much. But I am slightly worried about this 'looking after' business even though travelling is always easier with a companion, and she is delightful company. I quailed at the thought of the upset and disturbance of my own quiet travel arrangements. As she had insisted on doing her own booking and consequently we were not sitting together, I was able, when she boarded at the last minute with hair flying as usual but this time without the toothbrush to pretend, coward as I am, that she was nothing to do with me, while I noted that the only brush was with the aircrew who were told not to worry as they still had 'five minutes'.

I, of course, had boarded when I was told to and I heaved a sigh of relief as we took off.

So we arrived together in Delhi and thankfully, she was there to find the luggage, shout joyfully for Thompson, greet all around her and take us home.

It seemed like home this time, another home and utterly different from my own quiet existence. Everyone welcomed me, it was all familiar and I felt a part of it and part of the household. In a country where the elderly and Mothers-in-law are accepted and are part of the extended family the surprise is when I go away, not when I arrive. It was great to be back with the family once more. Even in a short time the young people had changed and circumstances had changed too - there was more going on, a constant stream of visitors of all age groups. I had friends from my last visit and a party seemed somehow to have started on my very first night. People gathered to say 'Hello' and added to my feeling of belonging.

It was pleasantly warm here and I thought of my theme of contrasts again as I had left behind endless raging winds whistling around the houses with a dreary refrain. There we had dug out and huddled into our overcoats, here summer clothes were still much in evidence.

The changes here had brought even more activity, there were constant comings and goings, young people arriving, our own departing, a visiting football team arrived (or was it basketball) for it is Jennie who takes on a "could-you-possibly-house-a-few" when they are playing an away match. It is also Jennie who obligingly says 'yes' to a "both-away-at-the-moment" left-behind child and it is Jennie who spends half the night at the airport with a forgot-to-confirm traveller who is stranded there and is desperately hoping to get on the departing plane. So it is Jennie who is at the hub of this lively happy bustle. It is not surprising, therefore, that this attitude extended to the staff and their associates.

"Life in your staff quarters appears to differ from life in other peoples' establishments," I said to Simon, "it's great, I know, but what happens when you go?"

"It'll work out," he replies vaguely waving his hands.

The staff quarters seem as full and as active as the main house, whether all these people work here is doubtful and 'family' here seems to include a large number of dependants. There is Munju's mother for example, she had arrived from the hills to avoid the snowy winter. Like me she doesn't like the cold, but unlike me, who only had a few aches and pains, she appeared to be very ill, I was told she had 'fever' but this vague term could mean anything so I was no wiser. I enquired after her at regular intervals and at one time Munju went into such graphic details speaking fast, waving her hands around her body and ending at the feet that I had the unpleasant thought of 'feet first' and I prepared to give sympathy and even, perhaps, attend a Hindu funeral. While this was passing through my mind I saw that Munju was smiling broadly when she said 'Better'. I wondered about the body movements, perhaps the ailment had passed out through the feet or perhaps, like my own family, hers thought a good walk was the answer to all problems and would do her good. Then I saw that she had come out of hiding and was sitting in the garden in a small patch of sunlight. I noticed that one foot was red and swollen and I learned later from Munju that on the way to hospital a scooter had hit her and knocked her down, this is a dangerous place and I was sorry when I came to think about the accident that she had had to walk to hospital in her feverish state. A decision came to me that of improving Munju's English while I was here so that I could be informed of such events. I thought it more likely that I could improve Munju's English than I could master Hindi.

I was called to another small crisis on my first morning which I was hoping would be a peaceful one; my room, on the ground floor, has large french windows and I could see that there was some agitation without. The daytime chokidar was standing there with others pointing to him and to his head, I waved hopefully but although I was quite aware that my attention was needed I tried to ignore the drama. Eventually there was much knocking at my door and Thompson, who has the best English, was sent to me. The chokidar was ill. "Fever," said Thompson.

"What sort of fever?" I asked.

"Very hot sort, very hot head, head hurts," he explained, "Fever," he said again, firmly this time. Even I should know fever.

I found paracetamol but explained that it was not good for Malaria or Dengue fever.

"It will help his head," I told Thompson, "he can go home."

This produced more alarm as he didn't want to go home, I realised later that if he went home he would lose pay so it was no use my trying to get a replacement. My role was to supply the pain-killers while the rest of the staff manned the gate until the evening guard took over. There seemed to be a lot more 'staff' than usual and even Thompson took his turn. I was impressed with the fellowship here that made this effort possible. He rested and told me he was better but when the evening chokidar took over he, at last, went home and didn't return for a week.

"What was the matter?" I asked Munju.

"Fever," she replied.

The kitchen often seemed to be the heart of social activity, I recognised the sweeper and the Mali.

"Ah," I said to the Mali, "where is my banana tree?" My tone was accusing.

This was a precious cutting I had managed to obtain from a government nursery, it had cost me about the equivalent of 25p and I had potted it up and talked to it daily, its pot was now empty.

The Mali grinned broadly and said, "Come". He led me to the bottom of the garden where a large banana tree flourished.

"Is this it?" I was astounded.

"Yes, yes, planted in garden, not in pot. Very good banana tree."

Well, well, perhaps next year? Who knows.

The main house is like Waterloo station, with the constant activity, it must be confusing for Hari and Munju because there could be a dozen or more milling around about supper time so they would expect a party and start to prepare for it, then suddenly all would be quiet and three would sit down for the meal of plenty.

"It'll come in for lunch," Simon would say philosophically, cheerfully and perhaps thoughtfully at the unusual peace and quiet.

I saw that he had made a new office at the top of the stairs on the landing, the computer and usual equipment was no longer in his bedroom, a useful move if he or Jennie ever needed sleep, the computer was very popular. Other rooms were often overflowing, sometimes the bedrooms or even the sitting room looked like a dormitory and the bedrooms would be empty, I supposed these guests and our own had just sat there and fallen asleep.

Party-time arrived and Liz decided on the sort of 'do' that needed a shamiyana (large colourful tent). I was out when this went up but it looked very impressive and the lawn was covered in carpets. Fortunately for me my bedroom was on the other side of the house but the neighbourhood must have had the advantage of the musical entertainment.

"I think I have a slight headache," said Simon next morning, he was reading a note from Liz that said, 'Leave the mess, I'll clear it up later' - 'in the morning' was crossed out.

Most of the party must have gone home in the early hours but various groups kept emerging so that breakfast, or whatever the meal was, went on for a long time. No Liz.

"Let's go for a walk," said Simon. Jennie agreed.

I stayed to watch the removal of the shamiyana. I'd expected a large lorry but the men arrived on a bicycle, admittedly it had been fitted with a sort of box on the back but it still looked an inadequate conveyance. The whole process of dismantling was more African than Indian in its speed although I had to admit it was efficient enough. The obvious boss sat on a table and all the collection of poles, canvas and carpet was transported a bit at a time on the man-powered vehicle.

The lawn looked a mess and the poor Mali had been working on it for a week. It never did look like an English bowling green and now it looked even less like.

How different the office party and again I think of my contrast - theme. This party was a lunchtime affair and everyone was sedately sober and well dressed, the gentle Indian ladies looked lovely and everyone was on their best behaviour. I remembered an office party in Zambia years ago (another contrast here) when riotous African dancing along with an inexhaustible supply of local beer had even me learning some bottom waggling that is not my general behaviour. I remember Jennie and I hiding away the more expensive drink as the hip swaying changed to forgetfulness and bodies lay in the garden. I think that I can no longer imagine Simon and Jennie enjoying this violent exuberance. I remember with some regret but now view the sedate serene and beautifully draped Indian ladies and think what a well run and tranquil office theirs must be.

The Christmas party this year was a family and neighbourly affair, good food and even some poetry reading, the young people left early having been quietly polite.

I had made friends last year with Claire and David, a marvellously independent couple and the parents of a friend. I wonder why I thought I could be a help when they expressed a wish to visit Shimla. Was it perhaps because I'd been there before? There are so many places I haven't visited that another trip into the hills was surely one I should have gracefully declined. I suppose I was showing off but the deciding factor was the arrival of Victoria bent on seeing as much as she could in three weeks.

It hadn't changed at the Station, there were the usual and almost unbelievable crowds there and here independence is a mistake.

Porters will shoulder everything, they know the station, the platforms, the trains and will find your seat before holding out their hopeful hands and their red shirts and turbans make them unmistakable. I was not happy without at least one of them especially as the loudspeaker voice changed us about from platform to platform and I cannot read the small print which is stuck on the side of the carriage to tell travellers the seat numbers. The train was late, it arrived at the junction to change to the mountain train at midnight, we had three hours in a freezing hotel and six hours next morning sitting in the little train that didn't go. I need my sleep but Vicky, bless her, did find us some tea. I was too tired to appreciate the toy train again and was thankful when we arrived at last at Shimla. I wasn't being much use to anybody, I was much too cold and my nose was bleeding.

We all went down into the town next day and I explained airily that I had no trouble getting back as I just took a taxi. David, an ex-naval commander took out his compass. This proved to be a wise move as Vicky and I, two taxis later, were still unaware of where we were as was the taxi driver. He pointed upwards, "Now, foot," he said, "fifty rupees."

"Don't pay him," said Vicky slamming the taxi door and looking furiously about us. But I was weak and glad to be rid of this man who seemed not to know his own town.

I paid him, we took to 'foot' and fell in with a delightful man who showed us the way and asked us to tea. We didn't go.

"Sisters?" he asked us. Such a nice man! We laughed our way to the hotel where Claire and David has been for hours.

We tried to visit the Yak next day but the park was closed so even Yaks have a day off. The horses were still there but I gave up any ideas of pony trekking. It had been a lovely thought.

I think this bit should be entitled, "Why the hell did you bring Grandma?"

"It was interesting," said Vicky later, "especially when we arrived at the wrong station in Delhi."

It was cold in Delhi too, and thick fog descended, shawls and woolly hats came out, I hadn't left the cold of England for this. Flights were cancelled, traffic slowed up and lights seemed to be of little use.

"It's unusual," everybody said as they huddled into various wrappings. In the town I saw a baby bundled up in woolly jumpers and hat but with nothing on its lower half showing a pretty brown bare bottom. No nappy washing needed and there is always a shortage of water in some parts of the town.

When the weather improved Simon said, "I haven't forgotten Bharatpur, Claire and David will join us, I'll book us all in. We know a good hotel.

It was an old palace and reeked of past wealth, it was built, as so many of these palaces are, around a courtyard and there were fires and a fountain. The magnificence of the hotel was enhanced by the wonderful furniture all part of the same period with four-poster beds, antiquated desks, wardrobes, chairs and tables. I wondered what the agent from the firm who lets my cottage would have thought of this with his love of uniformity and a 'this-cupboard-will-make-a-shower' attitude. I wished he could see the huge, ornamental, solid doors, the high painted ceilings, the tiled patios with enormous copper pots and the great painted archways around the balcony that overlooked the courtyard. At night we sat around the sweet smelling wood fires there, while we were entertained by an Indian Puppet show.

Just briefly I thought of my contrasts and the awful poverty of back street Delhi, had this inequality always existed?

We were here to see the wild life park called Keoladeo Sanctuary where there are said to be over four hundred different kinds of birds. It was this place that Simon had written to me about, it must be one of the most spectacular breeding and feeding grounds in the world. Originally developed as a shooting preserve it has now been a sanctuary for some years. There are other animals for we saw two python and some spotted deer, I think I remember wild pigs but I'm not sure.

We saw among the other thousands of birds, the Siberian Crane now almost extinct. The guides, who also rode the bicycle rickshaws, were very knowledgeable as Simon had told me. We hired these rickshaws and the guide told us of their training which was considerable. These vehicles can go almost anywhere but there are walking trails too, but, thankfully, no cars. I think my favourite bird was the kingfisher, I had never before seen so many. I marvelled at the amount of food there must be in these marshes and lakes to feed the thousands of birds. This is the most wonderful place to visit if one is at all interested in birds.

I slept well in my spacious room which had equally spacious facilities. Plenty of room here to prance about if one felt so inclined. I felt I could spend weeks in a place like this and not tire of it.

We returned to Delhi and once more I thought of my theme of contrasts, for Delhi, or parts of it, are so overcrowded and we had viewed the extensive countryside. In Delhi, too, there is the magnificent beside the shoddy, the richness beside the poverty, the beauty beside the ugly and in the people the beautifully dressed beside the ragged filthy poor!

"You'll enjoy the hill fort hotels," said Simon, "we'll do a few trips now that the weather is better."

The weather had been steadily improving and I was always ready to see something different.

"Have you been to these two before?" I asked as I tried to glean some information from the books.

"Well, no," he replied, "but people are always going there, it'll be great." One drawback I found was that a hillfort hotel was on a hill.

"This is more like mountaineering," I complained as we left the car park which was on the flat.

"A hill fort is built so that the countryside all round can be surveyed," said Simon as we paused a moment in the climb, "the view at the top will be magnificent."

It was and that is true of any of these hotels though they varied in other details. One, where we stayed, was 'dry'. Simon went for refreshment in the evening and returned to us with the news that there was coke or lemonade.

"It's a hotel and there's no licence, I ask you?" We all had an immediate thirst as there is nothing like being told you can't to bring on an immediate desire.

We looked at each other, decided on the rock climbing again and went in search of a local wine bar. We noticed that other guests, better informed, had brought their own drink with them. Perhaps they also knew how unappetising the food was at this particular hotel, it was not geared to Indian palates and no American or European could say it was even mediocre. Viewing the mud coloured slushy pudding I asked for ice-cream. It came - it was warm.

The view was spectacular and the garden lovely.

"You have to take the rough with the smooth," said Simon, "but I think we'll report it when we get back other people ought to know what to expect."

As this is India and not Pakistan, it is unusual not to find a hotel licensed. Whether it was a new Muslim manager or if it was a 'dry' day or if they had just run out we never knew. The next day we moved on into the now brilliant sunshine and the sights of agricultural India. I counted a hundred camels with their great loads and saw vast numbers of mustard fields. We stayed at another fort with more climbing, lovely cold ice-cream and the same marvellous views.

"It looks as if Jaipur will be out this year," said Simon sorrowfully as we gazed out over the countryside.

"I'm going to Jaipur next week," said Julie, a young Mother friend who had joined us at this fort, she said it in an inviting sort of voice.

"Taking the baby," she added.

I waited expectantly.

"And the ayah, you'd be very welcome." I wasted no time in debate with myself.

"Great," I said, "When and how?"

Julie wasted no time either, when we returned she fixed up both train and hotel.

"It's not the best hotel," she told me, "it's the only one I could find with any vacancies."

She made it sound a bit sleazy but at least I wouldn't be paying the earth and funds were getting a bit low.

It wasn't sleazy in the least, it was another palace-turned-hotel but this was still in the process of conversion so was not outrageously expensive. We made an early start and I found that Julie had different ideas in porterage from the friends Vicky and I had travelled with earlier. They had been scornful of the very idea that help was needed. I justify my use of porters by thinking of the good I am doing. This time our need was so obvious they were worth their weight in gold as they shouldered and headed the baby carriage, the cot, a baby canteen and the dozen other packages that so small a person cannot travel without. My backpack looked insignificant. The tip is modest, for a few rupees it is not worth the effort of doing for oneself. The ayah hung on to the baby.

And so, after all, I visited the wonderful pink city of Jaipur. The hotel was full of atmosphere and I had another four-poster bed. The rooms were varied, Julie had new bathroom facilities and I had a television. The ayah had a tiger head that caused her to shudder and say that she couldn't sleep with it. Julie said, "You have no choice."

"But," said the ayah, "your room has two beds and I could look after the baby?"

"This is your room," said Julie, "just don't look at the tiger."

"I suppose I could change," I said, reluctantly, looking at my beautiful bed.

"No," said Julie "we're all fine," in a very positive way, "we'll have lunch and go sight-seeing."

I won't say more about this city, it's one of the musts for someone visiting India and is generally included in a package tour. I can't describe pink except to say that it is warm and friendly. In the sunshine the buildings glow in a welcoming sort of way. It is very beautiful.

The hotel garden, being the garden of an old palace, was large and full of peacocks. This was the India I had hoped for, we rested in this garden and later watched the filling of the new swimming pool. This is a necessity for tourism but it is sad that the atmosphere may soon be ruined as these needs take over and uniformity dominates. It may be more sanitary but it will certainly be more dull.

"How was Jaipur?" asked Simon when we returned. He didn't wait for a reply, "It's Ranthanbhore next year."

I keep on hoping.

Liz and a friend shot off to Pushkar one day.

"Bus," she said as she skimmed past me.

"Pushkar?" I said hopefully but I was obviously too late so I decided that the guide book would have to do me, plenty of information if little excitement. I'd developed the Delhi cough again and didn't think I could face an uncomfortable night on the bus - not that I was asked. Pushkar is the pace of the great camel fair and even a second-hand report would be better than nothing. However it was not the right time for this event. This didn't bother Liz and when she returned she was so full of the people, the kindness and the peace of the place that she hardly noticed such things as camels.

"I'll have to go back," she said, "I've left lots of orders." Liz loves shopping.

Orders? "Orders for what?" I asked.

Liz vaguely waved her hands - she was so full of her story.

"After Delhi," she said "it was so wonderful."

"Pushkar?" queried Simon as he, too, dashed past, "next year perhaps, let's see," he confirmed to me, "have you been to Ranthanbhore?"

I tried to point out that there might not be a next year but he gave me a look of 'what-are-you-talking-about-woman', so I subsided and tried not to cough. Once home this graveyard sound would disappear as I would breathe deeply of my clear sea air.

It's time to go when I begin to feel too much at home here. When I no longer notice cows laying in the middle of the road or all the stray dogs, the beggars and the rubbish. But most of all I know it is time to go when I start to find fault with the staff. This was happening.

"Hang on a minute," I told myself, "you won't have all this back home."

But I shall have tidy streets, wonderful green fields, traffic that obeys rules and a peaceful place where no-one will sweep dust about and make me cough.

Have I stayed too long? Already the market traders were beginning to welcome me as a known customer, one who would come again and not a mere passer by.

I start looking at the beautiful silks and saris and imagining myself in them. How unrealistic when I have to cope with a wild westerly, no flowing robes for me as I pull my anorak hood over my head and draw the strings tightly.

I pack and leave the silks behind. I shall not write "The End" this time. Anything could happen.